The route to

When they look back at their formative years, []l part Amar Chitra Katha picture books have pl [] r **Chitra Katha** – that first gave them a glimpse o []

Since they were introduced in 1967, there are now **over 400 Amar Chitra Katha** titles to choose from. **Over 100 million copies** have been sold worldwide.

Now the Amar Chitra Katha titles are even more widely available in **1000+ bookstores all across India**. Log on to www.ack-media.com to locate a bookstore near you. If you do not have access to a bookstore, you can buy all the titles through our online store **www.amarchitrakatha.com**. We provide quick delivery anywhere in the world.

To make it easy for you to locate the titles of your choice from our treasure trove of titles, the books are now arranged in six categories.

Epics and Mythology
Best known stories from the Epics and the Puranas

Indian Classics
Enchanting tales from Indian literature

Fables and Humour
Evergreen folktales, legends and tales of wisdom and humour

Bravehearts
Stirring tales of brave men and women of India

Visionaries
Inspiring tales of thinkers, social reformers and nation builders

Contemporary Classics
The Best of Modern Indian literature

Amar Chitra Katha Pvt Ltd
© Amar Chitra Katha Pvt Ltd, 1972, Reprinted April 2017,
ISBN 978-81-8482-218-2
Published by Amar Chitra Katha Pvt. Ltd., 201 & 202, Sumer Plaza,
2nd Floor, Marol Maroshi Road, Andheri (East), Mumbai- 400 059. India
Printed at Zirius Images Pvt. Ltd, Bhiwandi, Thane- 421 311.
For Consumer Complaints Contact Tel : +91-22 49188881/2/3
Email: customerservice@ack-media.com

The route to your roots

LOKAMANYA TILAK

'Swaraj is my birthright and I shall have it' -- this clarion call was given by Bal Gangadhar Tilak. He was a towering figure in the Indian Independence movement. A nationalist to the core, he believed strongly that modern education would inculcate patriotism and self-respect in the people. His inspiring speeches and writing landed Tilak in jail several times. But this did not dampen his spirit or will to cast off the yoke of foreign rule from his motherland.

Script
Indu J. Tilak

Illustrations
Dilip Kadam

Editor
Anant Pai

Cover illustration by: P. G. Sirur

LOKAMANYA TILAK

ON JULY 23, 1856, GANGADHAR PANT TILAK, THE HEADMASTER OF THE LOCAL MARATHI SCHOOL IN RATNAGIRI, WAS PACING UP AND DOWN THE VERANDA OF HIS HOUSE. HIS WIFE WAS ABOUT TO HAVE A BABY.

HE HAD THREE DAUGHTERS, BUT LIKE OTHER PARENTS OF HIS TIME HE LONGED FOR A SON.

IT'S A GIRL!

WHAT! ANOTHER DAUGHTER!

POOR, DADA! I WILL TELL HIM THE TRUTH.

AUNTY'S TEASING YOU, DADA! IT'S A BOY!

YES, IT IS. BUT DON'T BE JUBILANT AND INVITE BAD LUCK.

OH! HOW SUPERSTITIOUS CAN YOU GET! LIKE WHOM DOES HE LOOK?

WHOEVER HE LOOKED LIKE, THE CHILD, BAL GANGADHAR TILAK, WAS DESTINED TO BECOME GREAT

BAL HAD HIS EARLY EDUCATION AT HOME, UNDER THE STRICT SUPERVISION OF HIS FATHER.

DADA, THIS SUM IS TOO SIMPLE. GIVE ME A MORE DIFFICULT ONE.

LATER, MY SON. NOW WE'LL PRACTISE THE SANSKRIT SHLOKAS.

WHEN BAL WAS TEN YEARS OLD, HIS FATHER WAS TRANSFERRED TO PUNE.

THIS IS A GODSEND! BAL CAN NOW GO TO THE BEST OF SCHOOLS.

SHORTLY AFTER THEY CAME TO PUNE, BAL'S MOTHER DIED. IT WAS HIS AUNT WHO NOW LOOKED AFTER HIM.

BAL, YOU'VE FORGOTTEN YOUR SLATE.

BUT I DON'T NEED IT, AUNTY.

I CAN DO SUMS IN MY MIND.

I KNOW, I KNOW. BUT YOU MUST CARRY A SLATE. ALL THE OTHER BOYS DO.

BAL WAS NO DOUBT INTELLIGENT. BUT HE WAS, TO HIS TEACHER'S ANNOYANCE, EQUALLY STUBBORN. ONE DAY AT SCHOOL —

OH, NO! HE'S HERE! HE'S COME!

PUT AWAY THE PEANUTS! RUN TO YOUR SEATS! TAKE UP YOUR BOOKS!

THE TEACHER ENTERED AND TOOK ONE LOOK AT THE CLASS.

WHAT'S GOING ON HERE? YOU OUGHT TO BE ASHAMED OF YOURSELVES!

WHEN THE BOYS PRETENDED TO BE SORRY FOR WHAT THEY HAD DONE, THE TEACHER RELENTED.

ALL RIGHT. THIS TIME I'LL LET YOU OFF. NOW CLEAN UP THE MESS, AND GET BACK TO YOUR WORK.

AS THE BOYS BENT DOWN TO PICK UP THE SHELLS, THE TEACHER'S EYE FELL ON BAL.

HEY, YOU! DO YOU THINK YOU ARE A PRINCE? COME ON, GET TO WORK.

I'M SORRY, SIR, BUT I WON'T.

WHAT!

I DIDN'T EAT IN CLASS. I DIDN'T MAKE THE MESS. SO WHY SHOULD I TAKE THE PUNISHMENT?

YOU IMPUDENT, OBSTINATE CHILD! I'LL TEACH YOU TO TALK BACK TO YOUR TEACHER!

BEFORE YOU DO, I AM GOING HOME, SIR. I WILL NOT SUBMIT TO UNFAIR TREATMENT.

TRUTHFUL, FEARLESS, PROUD — SUCH WAS THE STUFF BAL WAS MADE OF.

HE JOINED ANOTHER SCHOOL. BUT THOUGH HE WAS AN EXCELLENT STUDENT HE DID NOT DO WELL IN EXAMINATIONS.

WHY DO YOU ALWAYS PICK THE MOST DIFFICULT QUESTIONS, BAL? IF YOU ANSWERED THE EASY ONES, YOU'D GET FULL MARKS!

IT'S NOT MARKS THAT I'M AFTER. IT'S KNOWLEDGE. SO THERE'S NO POINT IN ATTEMPTING WHAT I ALREADY KNOW.

WHEN BAL WAS FIFTEEN, HE WAS MARRIED TO A TEN-YEAR-OLD GIRL NAMED SATYABHAMA. CHILD MARRIAGE WAS COMMON IN THOSE DAYS.

HIS FATHER-IN-LAW WANTED TO BUY HIM A PRESENT.

WOULD YOU LIKE TO HAVE A GOLD RING, BAL?

IF YOU DON'T MIND, I'D PREFER BOOKS. THEY ARE MORE VALUABLE.

THAT SAME YEAR, BAL'S FATHER DIED.

BAL, YOU MUST GET OVER YOUR GRIEF AND CONCENTRATE ON YOUR STUDIES.

THAT'S WHAT DADA WOULD WANT ME TO DO. YES, I MUST GET OVER MY GRIEF, UNCLE.

AND GET OVER IT HE DID. HE WAS SEVENTEEN WHEN HE JOINED THE DECCAN COLLEGE. ON THE FIRST DAY AS THE BOYS ASSEMBLED AT THE MESS FOR LUNCH —

WELL, WELL, TILAK! HOW ORTHODOX CAN WE GET! A SILK DHOTI — IT REMINDS ME OF MY FATHER AND GRAND-FATHER!

HA! HA! HA!

THE BOY WHO HAD MADE THE COMMENT WAS DAJI ABAJI KHARE.

WHAT'S WRONG WITH IT? IT'S OUR TRADITIONAL DRESS! DON'T THE EURO-PEANS HAVE THEIR FORMAL DRESS FOR DINNERS?

SHABASH!

AFTER THE MEAL —

YOU ARE OUT-SPOKEN AREN'T YOU, TILAK? I HAVE MUCH TO LEARN FROM YOU.

AND, I, FROM YOU, KHARE.

LATER, ON THEIR WAY TO COLLEGE —

I WANT TO IMPROVE MY PHYSIQUE, KHARE.

COME TO THE GYM WITH ME, THEN. I'LL MAKE YOU A PEHLWAN.*

AND THUS BEGAN THE LIFELONG FRIENDSHIP OF TILAK AND KHARE.

ONE PUNCH AND YOU'LL FALL FLAT, TILAK!

DON'T BRAG, KHARE. I'VE JUST BEGUN BESIDES, I'LL LICK YOU IN SWIMMING.

* WRESTLER

OF ALL SPORTS, SWIMMING WAS BAL'S FAVOURITE. ONE DAY HE AMAZED KHARE BY FLOATING ON HIS BACK FOR HOURS WITH A LOAF OF BREAD HELD ALOFT IN ONE HAND.

SEE, KHARE, NOT A DROP OF WATER ON THIS LOAF!

TILAK'S STAMINA HOWEVER BELIED HIS FOOD HABITS.

DAL AND RICE FOR ME, AS USUAL.

NO, MY PEHLWAN. YOU CANNOT SURVIVE ON ONLY THAT NOW. YOU WILL EAT CHAPATIES, GHEE, CURDS, FRESH VEGETABLES...

...AND PLENTY OF MILK.

TILAK'S DIET AND HEALTH NO DOUBT IMPROVED. BUT WHEN THE F.Y. ARTS RESULTS WERE ANNOUNCED—

I'VE FAILED. HM··M··M··I HAVE ACHIEVED ONE GOAL—A ROBUST PHYSIQUE. BUT...

...AT THE COST OF MY OTHER GOAL. I'LL HAVE TO STRIKE A BALANCE BETWEEN BOOKS AND SPORTS.

AND SO WELL DID HE DO IT THAT HE WAS HONOURED BY THE BRILLIANT MATHEMATICIAN, PROF. CHHATRE HIMSELF. FOR, ONCE WHEN A STUDENT WENT TO THE PROFESSOR SEEKING HELP —

I'M BUSY JUST NOW... BUT WAIT! GO TO TILAK. HE WILL SOLVE IT FOR YOU WITH EASE.

NOT ALL THE PROFESSORS, HOWEVER, APPRECIATED TILAK'S SUPERIOR INTELLIGENCE.

MR. TILAK, WHY DON'T YOU TAKE DOWN NOTES WHEN I LECTURE?

I DON'T NEED TO, SIR. I HAVE MASTERED THE SANSKRIT PORTION ON MY OWN.

IT WAS THIS FRANKNESS THAT EARNED TILAK THE NICKNAME — MR. BLUNT.

NEVERTHELESS HIS WORDS CARRIED WEIGHT WITH HIS FELLOW STUDENTS. ONCE IN THE COLLEGE HOSTEL —

WE LOST OUR INDEPENDENCE BECAUSE OF DISUNITY...

YOU ARE WRONG. THE BRITISH TRICKED US INTO SLAVERY.

AND THE BOY REACHED OUT FOR THE PICTURE OF THE QUEEN OF ENGLAND, HANGING ON THE WALL.

WHAT ARE YOU DOING?

WHAT I OUGHT TO HAVE DONE MUCH EARLIER...

...TRAMPLING IT! THIS IS WHAT THE BRITISH DESERVE!

STOP IT! YOU... YOU...

...COWARD! DO YOU THINK THAT TRAMPLING A MERE PICTURE MAKES YOU A HERO?

DISPLAY YOUR LOVE OF FREEDOM IN A MORE WORTHY MANNER! HAMMER THE THRONE OF ENGLAND, IF YOU CAN! IF NOT, AT LEAST CHERISH SUCH AN AMBITION.

THE HERO MEEKLY HEARD HIM OUT!

SOON AFTER GRADUATING IN ARTS, TILAK TOOK UP THE STUDY OF LAW. AROUND THAT TIME HE STRUCK UP A FRIENDSHIP WITH GOPAL GANESH AGARKAR, AN M.A. STUDENT, AND A BUDDING CHAMPION OF SOCIAL REFORMS.

WITHOUT EDUCATING THE PEOPLE, WE CANNOT HOPE TO INTRODUCE SOCIAL REFORMS.

I DON'T SEE WHAT IMPACT SOCIAL REFORMS IMPOSED BY AN ALIEN GOVERNMENT CAN HAVE ON THE PEOPLE?

WE MUST HAVE POLITICAL FREEDOM FIRST!

BUT EVEN THAT CANNOT BE ACHIEVED WITHOUT MODERN EDUCATION!

THERE I AGREE WITH YOU!

THE IDEA WAS SOON PUT INTO SHAPE. WITH THE HELP OF VISHNUSHASTRI CHIPLUNKAR, THE TWO FRIENDS FOUNDED A SCHOOL.

PEOPLE REFER TO IT AS THE NEW SCHOOL. LET'S NAME IT 'THE NEW ENGLISH SCHOOL.'

THE NIGHT BEFORE THE INAUGURATION AS TILAK AND HIS CLOSE FRIEND NAMJOSHI WERE GOING THE ROUNDS—

HOW CAN WE EXPECT THE CHILDREN TO SIT ON THIS JAGGED FLOOR, TILAK?

LET'S LEVEL IT OUT, THEN.

THE TWO FRIENDS WORKED HARD.

AT THE END OF IT THEY WERE SO EXHAUSTED THAT...

...THEY FELL ASLEEP IN THE SCHOOL, WITH A BLACK BOARD FOR A BED!

THE SCHOOL ATTRACTED THE BEST OF TALENTS. SUCH AN ENCOURAGING RESPONSE INSPIRED THE FRIENDS TO WORK WITH GREATER ENTHUSIASM.

WE'RE LUCKY TO CATCH THEM YOUNG. AND IF WE DON'T SUCCEED IN INCULCATING SELF-RESPECT AND LOVE FOR THE COUNTRY IN THEM...

WE WILL SUCCEED! IF ONLY WE COULD REACH THE ADULTS TOO!

TILAK'S WORDS SET CHIPLUNKAR THINKING. ONE DAY —

I'VE FOUND A WAY TO REACH THE ADULTS! WHY DON'T WE START A WEEKLY?

WHY ONE, LET'S HAVE TWO! ONE IN ENGLISH AND THE OTHER IN MARATHI!

TILAK! NONE OF US HAVE THE JOURNALISTIC EXPERIENCE FOR ONE, AND YOU TALK OF TWO.

BUT, AGARKAR, YOU HAVE MUCH TO SAY. YOUR HEART IS BURNING WITH PATRIO- TISM! WORDS WILL FLOW OF THEIR OWN ACCORD!

AND SO THE TWO WEEKLIES—KESARI IN MARATHI AND THE MAHRATTA IN ENGLISH WERE BORN.

THERE! OUR OFFICE! THE EDITOR'S CHAIR, DESK AND STATIONERY!

WHAT ABOUT THE PRINTING MACHINE, NAMJOSHI?

LEAVE THAT TO ME, AGARKAR.

NAMJOSHI MADE ARRANGEMENTS FOR A SECOND-HAND PRINTING MACHINE AND HAD IT SMUGGLED INTO THE SCHOOL ONE NIGHT.

SHH! WE DON'T WANT TO WAKE ANYONE!

SINCE THEY COULDN'T AFFORD A MECHANIC, TILAK SET IT UP.

DO YOU THINK WE'LL FINISH PRINTING IT IN TIME?

WE MUST, NAMJOSHI. THE COPIES MUST REACH THE PEOPLE EARLY IN THE MORNING.

BEFORE THE BREAK OF DAY, TILAK AND HIS FRIENDS THEMSELVES DISTRIBUTED COPIES FROM DOOR TO DOOR.

HAVE YOU READ TODAY'S KESARI...

I HAVE. THERE WAS SOMETHING ABOUT THE DIWAN OF KOLHAPUR.

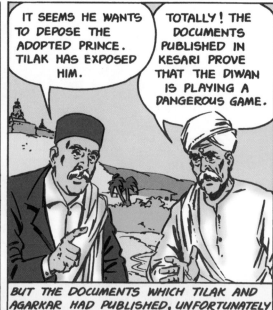

IT SEEMS HE WANTS TO DEPOSE THE ADOPTED PRINCE. TILAK HAS EXPOSED HIM.

TOTALLY! THE DOCUMENTS PUBLISHED IN KESARI PROVE THAT THE DIWAN IS PLAYING A DANGEROUS GAME.

BUT THE DOCUMENTS WHICH TILAK AND AGARKAR HAD PUBLISHED, UNFORTUNATELY TURNED OUT TO BE FABRICATED.

THE DIWAN SUED THE EDITORS AND HAD THEM JAILED IN SPITE OF THE APOLOGY OFFERED.

THE DOCUMENTS MAY BE FALSE, BUT I HAVE NO DOUBT THAT THE DIWAN IS UP TO SOME MISCHIEF.

ANYWAY TILAK AND AGARKAR DON'T DESERVE TO BE IMPRISONED FOR PUBLISHING WHAT THEY BELIEVED TO BE A GENUINE DOCUMENT.

THE VIEWS OF THE PEOPLE OF PUNE WERE OPENLY EXPRESSED IN THE ROUSING WELCOME GIVEN TO TILAK AND AGARKAR ON THEIR RELEASE FROM JAIL.

SOON AFTER THEIR RELEASE, THE FRIENDS FORMED THE DECCAN EDUCATION SOCIETY AND THE FERGUSSON COLLEGE WAS STARTED.

ONE GREAT THING ABOUT TILAK IS THAT WHILE HE ENCOURAGES MODERN EDUCATION, HE RESPECTS OUR CUSTOMS WHICH MANY OF OUR REFORMERS DO NOT.

BUT THIS FAITH IN TILAK WAS PUT TO THE TEST, IN A RATHER MISCHIVOUS MANNER, BY ONE GOPALRAO JOSHI.

WE HAVE SEVERAL REFORMERS IN PUNE. I WONDER HOW MANY OF THEM HAVE THE COURAGE TO PRACTISE WHAT THEY PREACH.

JOSHI INVITED THEM TO DELIVER LECTURES AT A CHRISTIAN MISSION. AFTER THE LECTURE —

SHALL WE LEAVE?

YOU CAN'T LEAVE WITHOUT HAVING A CUP OF TEA.

THE FOLLOWING DAY, THE ORTHODOXY WERE IN FOR A SHOCK.

DID YOU SEE THE MORNING PAPERS? RANADE AND GOKHALE, I CAN UNDERSTAND. BUT TILAK! I NEVER DREAMT THAT TILAK WOULD HAVE TEA FROM A CHRISTIAN KITCHEN!

GOPALRAO HAD SEEN TO IT THAT THEIR NAMES WERE PUBLISHED IN THE NEWSPAPERS!

ALL THIS REFORM BUSINESS IS GOING TOO FAR!

YES. WE MUST EXPEL THEM FROM THE COMMUNITY UNLESS THEY ARE PREPARED TO PERFORM THE PURIFICATION CEREMONY.

LATER, AT TILAK'S HOME —

PLEASE AGREE TO PERFORM THE CEREMONY.

NO! I WON'T. IS MY RELIGION SO FRAGILE THAT IT CAN BE POLLUTED BY A CUP OF TEA FROM A CHRISTIAN'S HOUSE?

NO PRIEST HAS AGREED TO COME TO OUR HOUSE FOR YOUR FATHER'S SHRADDHA* CEREMONY.

DON'T WORRY. BALAM BHATTA WILL NOT LET YOU DOWN.

VISHWANATH, HIS ELDEST SON, WAS CURIOUS.

WHO IS BALAM BHATTA, DADA?

YOU'LL SEE HIM TOMORROW.

OH! SO DADA IS BALAM BHATTA, THE PRIEST.

FOR TILAK, HIMSELF A SCHOLAR OF SANSKRIT, THE NON-COOPERATION OF PRIESTS POSED NO PROBLEM.

HE KNEW THE VEDAS BETTER THAN THEY DID. AND THE MORE HE DELVED INTO THE VEDAS THE MORE CURIOUS HE BECAME ABOUT THEIR ANTIQUITY.

THE HYMNS WHICH SUGGEST THE POSITION OF THE SUN AND THE CONSTELLATIONS SHOULD THROW LIGHT ON THE AGE OF THE VEDAS.

BASED ON ASTRONOMICAL EVIDENCE TILAK ESTABLISHED THE PERIOD OF THE VEDAS AS 4000 B.C.

EVEN IN THE MIDST OF ALL HIS SCHOLARLY PURSUITS, TILAK HAD NOT FORGOTTEN THE COMMON MAN.

THE MASSES MUST BE EDUCATED ABOUT THEIR RIGHTS. THE FIRST STEP IS TO FIND A FORUM FOR BRINGING PEOPLE OF VARIOUS COMMUNITIES TOGETHER.

* DEATH ANNIVERSARY

TO ACHIEVE THIS, HE SET THE TRADITION OF PUBLICLY CELEBRATING THE GANESHA FESTIVAL.

LATER HE CELEBRATED THE BIRTH ANNIVERSARY OF SHIVAJI AT RAIGAD, WHICH HAD ONCE BEEN THE CAPITAL OF THE MARATHAS.

SHIVAJI LOVED HIS COUNTRY AND HIS FREEDOM. HE WAS SELF-RESPECTING, COURAGEOUS, BRAVE AND NOBLE. LET HIS LIFE BE AN EXAMPLE TO ALL OF US.

AROUND THAT TIME, THE GOVERNMENT RAISED THE TAX* ON INDIAN CLOTH, TO HELP THE CLOTH FROM BRITAIN TO SELL BETTER.

FOR SWADESHI† CLOTH, IT'S TOO EXPENSIVE! WHY SHOULD WE BUY IT WHEN IMPORTED CLOTH IS AVAILABLE FOR THE SAME PRICE?

IT'S THE NEW TAX. WE ARE HELPLESS. WHAT CAN WE DO?

TILAK, HOWEVER, DID NOT SIT BACK HELPLESS.

IF WE DON'T BUY SWADESHI CLOTH, WHO WILL? HOW WILL OUR PEOPLE, OUR TRADE SURVIVE? IF YOU LOVE YOUR COUNTRY AND YOUR PEOPLE, DON'T BUY BRITISH CLOTH! BOYCOTT IT!

* EXCISE DUTY   † INDIGENOUS

ONCE WHEN FAMINE BROKE OUT IN MAHARASHTRA —

THE FARMERS ARE LEAVING THEIR VILLAGES! I MUST REACH THEM! INSTIL COURAGE INTO THEM! THEY MUST KNOW WHAT THEIR RIGHTS IN THEIR HOMELAND ARE!

TILAK DID NOT BELIEVE IN SENDING PETITIONS TO THE GOVERNMENT AS SOME OF HIS COLLEAGUES IN THE INDIAN NATIONAL CONGRESS, THE MODERATES, DID. HIS METHODS WERE DIFFERENT.

THE CROPS HAVE FAILED AND YOU HAVE NEITHER FOOD NOR MONEY. ARE YOU GOING TO LOSE THE ROOF ABOVE YOUR HEAD TOO? YOU HAVE A RIGHT TO LIVE! CAN'T YOU FIGHT FOR YOUR RIGHTS EVEN IN THE GRIP OF DEATH?

TILAR AND HIS SUPPORTERS WERE LABELLED EXTREMISTS. BUT THAT DID NOT DETER HIM.

GO BACK TO YOUR VILLAGES AND MAKE THE FARMERS CLAMOUR FOR FOOD AND FODDER. LET THE CLAMOUR PERSIST TILL THE DEAF GOVERNMENT HEARS THE CRY!

WE WILL NOT REST TILL THE CRY IS HEARD!

YOUNG AND OLD, TILAK'S VOLUNTEERS WENT TO THE VILLAGES CARRYING HIS MESSAGE.

FIGHT FOR YOUR RIGHTS! DON'T BE AFRAID OF PETTY OFFICIALS! NO ONE CAN COMPEL YOU TO SELL YOUR LAND TO PAY TAXES. INSTEAD, THE GOVERNMENT MUST HELP YOU IN SUCH TIMES!

THE OFFICIALS RETALIATED BY ARRESTING THE VOLUNTEERS. AT PENN A FURIOUS MOB SURROUNDED THE MAGISTRATE.

WHEN TILAK RUSHED TO THE SCENE —

BAL GANGADHAR TILAK KI JAI!

PEACE! PEACE, MY FRIENDS! I'LL SPEAK TO THE MAGISTRATE. LEAVE THE MATTER TO ME.

THE MOB MELTED AWAY. SUCH WAS THE SPELL CAST BY TILAK!

WHILE TILAK WAS BUSY WITH THE STRUGGLE TO SECURE FAMINE RELIEF FOR THE FARMERS, THE PLAGUE STRUCK PUNE. THE GOVERNMENT WAS AT FIRST INDIFFERENT AND TOOK NO MEASURES TO ARREST THE SPREAD OF THE DREADED DISEASE.

FINALLY WHEN IT DID ACT, IT DID SO WITH A VENGEANCE. ONE CHARLES RAND WAS APPOINTED PLAGUE COMMISSIONER.

I WANT EVERY HOUSE IN PUNE DISINFECTED. PUT ANYONE WHO IS ILL IN HOSPITAL AND TAKE THE RELATIVES TO THE CAMP OUTSIDE THE TOWN — BY FORCE IF NECESSARY. THAT'S ALL. YOU MAY GO.

BUT THERE WAS TROUBLE AFOOT.

OUR PEOPLE DON'T HAVE ANY TRUST IN THE SOLDIERS. AND I DON'T BLAME THEM. THE SOLDIERS ARE BRUTAL.

THEY DO NOT UNDERSTAND THE FEARS OF OUR PEOPLE. I'LL SEE WHAT I CAN DO ABOUT IT.

TILAK WENT THE ROUNDS, SOMETIMES WITH THE SOLDIERS, SOMETIMES ALONE.

YOUR SON IS DOWN WITH THE PLAGUE. IT IS YOUR DUTY TO SEND HIM TO THE ISOLATION HOSPITAL.

NO! NO! THAT MEANS SURE DEATH! I WANT MY SON TO REMAIN IN MY HOUSE. I WILL NOT...

PLEASE LISTEN TO ME, KAKA*. TO SAVE HIS LIFE AND THE LIVES OF OTHERS AT HOME, YOU MUST SEND HIM TO THE HOSPITAL.

YOU KNOW BEST, BALWANTRAO. DO AS YOU WISH.

* UNCLE

TILAK RAISED HIS VOICE AGAINST INHUMAN TREATMENT METED OUT TO THE SUFFERING PEOPLE OF PUNE. IN HIS ENGLISH WEEKLY, MAHRATTA, HE WROTE —

THE PLAGUE IS MORE MERCIFUL TO US THAN ITS HUMAN PROTOTYPE NOW REIGNING IN THE CITY...

HOW RIGHT TILAK IS! THEY CAUSE MORE MISERY THAN THE DISEASE DOES.

TILAK SET UP HIS OWN SEGREGATION CAMP FOR THE TERRIFIED VICTIMS AND THEIR RELATIVES. HE EVEN STARTED A FREE KITCHEN FOR THE POOR IN THE CAMP.

ALL THE LEADERS HAVE FLED, LEAVING US TO THE MERCY OF THE PLAGUE AND THE SOLDIERS. TILAK ALONE HAS STOOD BY US.

HE IS THE REAL LEADER.

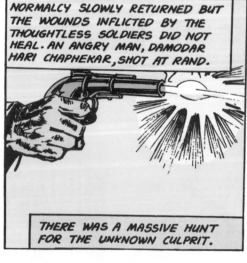

NORMALCY SLOWLY RETURNED BUT THE WOUNDS INFLICTED BY THE THOUGHTLESS SOLDIERS DID NOT HEAL. AN ANGRY MAN, DAMODAR HARI CHAPHEKAR, SHOT AT RAND.

THERE WAS A MASSIVE HUNT FOR THE UNKNOWN CULPRIT.

MEANWHILE, THE GOVERNMENT IMPOSED HEAVY FINES ON THE CITIZENS.

LOOK! LISTEN TO WHAT TILAK HAS TO SAY. HAS THE GOVERNMENT LOST ITS SENSES? TO RULE DOES NOT MEAN TO INDULGE IN REPRISALS.

TILAK IS WISE. BUT WILL THE GOVERNMENT SEE IT IN THAT LIGHT?

THEY CERTAINLY DIDN'T.

THE TIMES OF INDIA* ALLEGES THAT THE CULPRIT DREW INSPIRATION FROM TILAK'S WRITINGS AND SPEECHES.

THE ENGLISHMEN ARE SO PANIC-STRICKEN THAT THEY SEE MURDERERS EVEN IN THEIR OWN SHADOWS!

WHEN RAND DIED OF THE BULLET WOUND, THE ENGLISHMEN STEPPED UP THEIR CAMPAIGN AGAINST TILAK. FINALLY THE GOVERNMENT SWUNG INTO ACTION.

TILAK HAS BEEN ARRESTED.

THE GOVERNMENT HAS LOST ITS SENSES.

TILAK WAS HELD ON A CHARGE OF SEDITION.

DOES PRAISING SHIVAJI MAHARAJ AMOUNT TO SEDITION? TILAK HAS TAUGHT US TO FIGHT FOR OUR RIGHTS. IS THAT SEDITION?

HE HAS SHOWN US THE WAY TO GET GRIEVANCES REDRESSED LAWFULLY. IS THAT SEDITION?

WE OPENLY DARE TO CRITICISE THE GOVERNMENT. A FEW YEARS AGO WE COULD NOT EVEN THINK OF SUCH A THING!

THAT'S PRECISELY WHAT THE GOVERNMENT HAS AGAINST TILAK. HE HAS INSTILLED COURAGE INTO US. THAT IS SEDITION ACCORDING TO THEM.

* THEN CONTROLLED BY A BRITISH COMPANY

21

SOME OF HIS FRIENDS HINTED THAT TILAK SHOULD OFFER AN APOLOGY AND SECURE HIS RELEASE. TILAK REFUSED.

MY POSITION AMONG THE PEOPLE ENTIRELY DEPENDS UPON MY CHARACTER; AND IF I AM COWED DOWN BY THE PERSECUTION, I THINK, LIVING IN MAHARASHTRA IS AS GOOD AS LIVING IN THE ANDAMANS*.

AS EXPECTED THE COURT FOUND TILAK GUILTY. THE SENTENCE WAS EIGHTEEN MONTHS' RIGOROUS IMPRISONMENT. WHEN THE NEWS REACHED HIS WIFE, SHE FELL SERIOUSLY ILL.

BEG THE GOVERNMENT TO IMPRISON ME TOO! I HAVE BEEN HIS PARTNER IN EVERYTHING.

TILAK TOO FELL ILL IN PRISON. HE LOST 21 POUNDS!

HOWEVER, A MUSLIM WARDER TRIED TO BE OF HELP TO HIM.

DADASAHEB, I KNOW YOU DON'T LIKE FOOD COOKED WITH ONION AND GARLIC. HAVE SOME BETEL NUT. IT MIGHT HELP.

YOU ARE KIND BUT YOU ARE BREAKING PRISON RULES. YOU SHOULDN'T.

THE NEXT DAY, HE BROUGHT SOME COPRA AND JAGGERY. TILAK DECIDED TO LIE TO PUT HIM OFF.

I CAN'T EAT THESE. I HAVE A SORE MOUTH.

I'LL GET YOU ALMONDS AND SUGAR CANDY THEN.

TILAK HAD TO ACCEPT DEFEAT BEFORE SUCH PERSISTENCE.

*WHERE POLITICAL PRISONERS USED TO BE DEPORTED

WHEN TILAK WAS SHIFTED FROM BOMBAY TO YERAVDA JAIL, CHAPHEKAR WHO HAD BEEN CAUGHT AND SENTENCED TO DEATH, TOOK SPECIAL PERMISSION TO MEET HIM IN HIS CELL.

BALWANTRAO, I WANT TO DIE WITH THE GITA IN MY HAND. WILL YOU GIVE ME YOUR COPY?

WITH PLEASURE!

HE MIGHT HAVE BEEN MISGUIDED IN KILLING RAND. BUT CAN ANYONE DOUBT HIS PATRIOTISM?

A FEW DAYS LATER, A BENGALI GENTLEMAN CALLED ON TILAK.

PROF. MAX MUELLER HAS SENT YOU A GIFT — HIS TRANSLATION OF THE RIG VEDA. HE IS TRYING HIS BEST TO HAVE YOU RELEASED.

I AM HONOURED AND GRATEFUL.

THE RARE GIFT FROM THE FAMOUS GERMAN SCHOLAR WON FOR TILAK FACILITIES FOR READING AND WRITING IN HIS CELL.

ONE OF THE VERSES HE CAME ACROSS WHILE READING THE TRANSLATION MADE HIM PAUSE AND THINK.

"MANY DAYS PASSED BEFORE THE SUN ROSE." HOW COULD THIS BE TRUE... UNLESS...

... UNLESS THE ARYANS HAD ONCE LIVED IN THE ARCTIC! YES! THAT'S IT! IT HAS TO BE!

IT WAS THIS IDEA THAT LATER LED HIM TO WRITE THE BOOK — THE ARCTIC HOME IN THE VEDAS.

AT LAST ON SEPTEMBER 6, 1898, TILAK WAS RELEASED. THE TEMPLE BELLS OF PUNE RANG OUT ECHOING THE JOY OF THE PEOPLE.

FIVE YEARS LATER, THE PLAGUE BROKE OUT AGAIN IN PUNE. THIS TIME IT CLAIMED TILAK'S ELDEST SON.

WHY, OH WHY DIDN'T FATE SPARE VISHWANATH?

WHY SHOULD·IT? LIVES HAVE BEEN SNATCHED AWAY FROM SEVERAL HOMES. ONE WAS SNATCHED FROM OURS TOO.

BEARING HIS GRIEF WITH STOICISM, TILAK WORKED WITH EXTRA ZEAL.

THEN IN JULY 1905, LORD CURZON ANNOUNCED THE PARTITION OF BENGAL. THE PARTITION CAME INTO FORCE ON OCTOBER 16, 1905.

THEIR AIM IS TO DISUNITE THE BENGALI MUSLIMS AND HINDUS.

BUT THEY WILL NOT SUCCEED.

TILAK'S PREDICTION PROVED TRUE.

THE PARTITION ONLY GAVE FURTHER IMPETUS TO THE SWADESHI MOVEMENT. IN PUNE AS IN THE REST OF INDIA, PEOPLE BOYCOTTED FOREIGN GOODS. STUDENTS MADE A HUGE BONFIRE OF FOREIGN CLOTHES; THE FIRST OF MANY TO COME.

TILAK STARTED A GLASS FACTORY AT TALEGAON AND A CO-OPERATIVE STORE FOR THE SALE OF SWADESHI GOODS IN BOMBAY.

OUR RULERS ARE TRADERS AS WELL AS POLITICIANS. IF THE ONE IS PRESSED THE OTHER IS BOUND TO BE AFFECTED! IF WE ARE SELF-RELIANT WE WILL BECOME POLITICALLY FREE.

SINCE SWARAJ WAS THE GOAL OF TILAK AND HIS FRIENDS, LIKE LALA LAJPATRAI OF PUNJAB AND AUROBINDO GHOSE OF BENGAL, THEY CAME TO BE KNOWN AS NATIONALISTS.

...YOUR FUTURE RESTS ENTIRELY IN YOUR HANDS. IF YOU MEAN TO BE FREE, YOU CAN BE FREE; IF YOU DO NOT, YOU WILL FALL AND BE FOREVER FALLEN...

THE GOVERNMENT TRIED IN VAIN TO CURB THE NATIONALISTS. LALA LAJPATRAI WAS DEPORTED TO MANDALAY IN BURMA. BUT —

. ...IF YOUR AGITATION STOPPED AS SOON AS ONE DEPORTATION TOOK PLACE, THE GOVERNMENT WOULD GET AWAY WITH THE IDEA THAT REPRESSION HAD TRIUMPHED.

WHEN LAJPATRAI WAS RELEASED IN NOVEMBER 1907 —

LAJPATRAI SHOULD BE MADE THE PRESIDENT OF THE SURAT CONGRESS.

THAT WOULD BE A FITTING REPLY TO THE GOVERNMENT!

THE MODERATES HOWEVER WANTED DR. RASHBEHARI GHOSH.

WHEN THE TWO PARTIES MET —

IF WE ELECT LAJPATRAI, IT'LL TEACH THE GOVERN-MENT A LESSON.

BUT WE CAN'T OPENLY CHALLENGE THE GOVERNMENT! THEY'LL STAMP US OUT.

AT THE CONGRESS SESSION IN SURAT, TILAK WAS NOT ALLOWED TO SPEAK BEFORE DR. GHOSH'S ELECTION.

I'VE A RIGHT TO ADDRESS THE DELEGATES. YOU CAN'T STOP ME!

BUT THEY DID AND THE CONGRESS SPLIT INTO TWO GROUPS.

THIS WILL NEVER DO. A HOUSE DIVIDED AGAINST ITSELF CANNOT STAND. WE ARE PLAYING INTO THE HANDS OF THE BRITISH. WE MUST REMAIN UNITED FOR OUR GOAL IS ONE.

THE EXPLOSION ECHOED THROUGH THE COUNTRY. THE GOVERNMENT SWUNG INTO ACTION AND SEVERAL JOURNALISTS WERE JAILED.

TILAK, I WANT TO GIVE YOU A TIP. THE GOVERNMENT IS PLANNING TO ARREST YOU.

WHAT DOES IT MATTER? THE WHOLE COUNTRY IS LIKE A VAST PRISON. THEY ARE NOW GOING TO CONFINE ME IN A SMALLER ONE.

AROUND THIS TIME, REVOLUTIONARIES WHO BELIEVED IN VIOLENCE BECAME ACTIVE. ON APRIL 30, 1908 THE FIRST BOMB WAS THROWN AT THE BRITISH RESIDENTS OF MUZAFFARPUR.

A FEW DAYS LATER, TILAK WAS ARRESTED. THE CHARGE WAS SEDITION; THE OFFENCE, AN ARTICLE HE HAD WRITTEN.

THE CASE AGAINST TILAK CAME UP BEFORE THE BOMBAY HIGH COURT. THE ADVOCATE-GENERAL QUOTED FROM THE ARTICLE TO PRESS HIS CLAIM THAT TILAK WAS GUILTY.

" THE BOMB PARTY HAS COME INTO EXISTENCE AS A RESULT OF THE OPPRESSION PRACTISED BY THE OFFICIAL CLASS ... THE RESPONSIBILITY FOR THIS CALAMITY MUST, THEREFORE, BE THROWN NOT ON POLITICAL AGITATION, WRITINGS, OR SPEECHES BUT ON THE THOUGHTLESSNESS AND THE OBSTINACY OF THE OFFICIAL CLASS."

TILAK CONTENDED THAT WHILE HE DEPLORED THE USE OF BOMBS THE ONLY WAY TO PREVENT SUCH OCCURRENCES WAS TO REFORM THE ADMINISTRATION. HE MADE A FERVENT APPEAL TO THE JURY.

...FOR ME IT CAN ONLY BE A MATTER OF A FEW YEARS, BUT FUTURE GENERATIONS WILL LOOK TO YOUR VERDICT AND SEE WHETHER YOU HAVE JUDGED WRONG OR RIGHT. THE VERDICT MAY LIKELY BE A MEMORABLE ONE IN THE HISTORY OF THE FREEDOM OF THE INDIAN PRESS...

WHEN THE JURY FOUND HIM GUILTY —

I MAINTAIN THAT I AM INNOCENT....IT MAY BE THE WILL OF PROVIDENCE THAT THE CAUSE WHICH I REPRESENT MAY PROSPER MORE BY MY SUFFER-INGS THAN BY MY REMAINING FREE.

TILAK WAS SENTENCED TO TRANSPORTATION FOR SIX YEARS. IN BOMBAY A SIX-DAY STRIKE WAS OBSERVED AND ALL THE TEXTILE MILLS WERE CLOSED.

THE POLICE FIRED INDISCRIMINATELY AT THE DEMONSTRATORS.

TILAK WAS DEPORTED TO MANDALAY. 'BANDE MATARAM' THE BENGALI WEEKLY, BID HIM A PATHETIC FAREWELL.

GO, TILAK, WHEREVER YOU MAY BE SENT TO CRUSH YOUR BODY... THE CANKER OF THE CHAINS WILL NOT ONLY EAT INTO YOUR LIMBS BUT ALSO INTO EVERY HEART OF THE COUNTRY TO STIR IT UP TO ITS DUTY. YOU HAVE FULFILLED YOUR MISSION...

TILAK SPENT FIVE YEARS AND EIGHT MONTHS IN MANDALAY. HIS SOLE COMPANIONS WERE BOOKS AND BIRDS.

HE BEGAN TO WRITE A TREATISE ON THE GITA — THE GITA RAHASYA*.

TILAK'S PROLONGED DETENTION TOTALLY UNNERVED HIS WIFE AND SHE DIED WHEN HE WAS IN MANDALAY. WHEN THE JAILOR CAME INTO TILAK'S CELL —

I'M SORRY. IT MUST BE A GREAT LOSS TO YOU.

ONE OF US HAD TO FACE THE OTHER'S DEATH. I AM GLAD IT IS I. I ONLY WISH I COULD HAVE BEEN WITH HER WHEN THE END CAME.

* THE SECRET OF THE GITA

ON JUNE 17, 1914 AT 2·00 A.M. THERE WAS A KNOCK AT GAIKWAD WADA, TILAK'S RESIDENCE.

WHO IS IT?

IT'S ME. THE MASTER OF THE HOUSE.

THE WHOLE HOUSEHOLD WOKE UP. TILAK WAS BACK!

THE NEWS SPREAD. FRIENDS CAME RUNNING TO HIS HOUSE. THEY TALKED TILL DAYBREAK.

TELL ME WHAT IS HAPPENING IN THE COUNTRY.

LALA LAJPATRAI, BIPIN CHANDRA PAL AND AUROBINDO HAVE GONE INTO SELF-IMPOSED EXILE. THE PRESS IS GAGGED. NATIONAL SCHOOLS ARE CLOSED.

SOME WELL-WISHERS TRIED TO DISSUADE TILAK FROM TAKING PART IN POLITICS.

DADA, GIVE UP POLITICS NOW AT LEAST. DEVOTE YOUR TIME TO LITERATURE.

WHAT! INDULGE IN LITERATURE WHEN THE COUNTRY IS ROTTING IN SLAVERY?

SOMEBODY HAS TO DO THE WORK I AM DOING. IF NO ONE DOES IT, THE BRITISH WILL RULE AS THEY LIKE.

TILAK TOOK UP THE CAUSE OF HOME RULE, THE PEOPLE'S RIGHT TO FORM THEIR OWN GOVERNMENT. HE TOURED ALL OVER INDIA AND SPOKE TO THE PEOPLE.

HOME RULE IS THE ONLY REMEDY. INSIST ON YOUR RIGHTS. INDIA IS YOUR OWN HOME, ISN'T IT?

THEN WHY NOT MANAGE IT YOURSELVES?

WE DO NOT ASK FOR SEPARATION FROM ENGLAND. BUT OUR DOMESTIC AFFAIRS MUST BE IN OUR HANDS.

IT MUST BE NOTED THAT TILAK DEMANDED ONLY HOME RULE, NOT TOTAL INDEPENDENCE. THE TIME WAS NOT YET RIPE FOR IT.

TILAK BY THEN HAD COME TO BE REVERED AS LOKAMANYA* BY PEOPLE ALL OVER INDIA. WHEN HE WENT TO LUCKNOW TO ATTEND THE CONGRESS SESSION, FOLLOWING THE UNIFICATION OF THE MODERATES AND NATIONALISTS, HE WAS TAKEN OUT IN PROCESSION.

LOKAMANYA TILAK KI JAI!

* RESPECTED BY THE PEOPLE

SOME ENTHUSIASTIC YOUTHS UNHARNESSED THE HORSES AND DREW THE CARRIAGE THEMSELVES.

VICTORY TO LOKAMANYA TILAK!

AT THE LUCKNOW CONGRESS—

SWARAJ IS MY BIRTHRIGHT AND I SHALL HAVE IT.

LATER, TILAK VISITED ENGLAND TO PRESENT INDIA'S CASE FOR HOME RULE...

...AND WON MANY FRIENDS, NOTABLY FROM THE LABOUR PARTY.

ON AUGUST 1, 1920, EXACTLY EIGHT MONTHS AFTER HIS RETURN TO INDIA, TILAK DIED. BUT THE CAUSE FOR WHICH HE FOUGHT WAS TAKEN UP BY MILLIONS OF HIS COUNTRYMEN.

BRITISHERS, QUIT INDIA!

AND TILAK'S LIFELONG STRUGGLE AT LAST BORE FRUIT ON AUGUST 15, 1947, WHEN INDIA BECAME INDEPENDENT.

CELEBRATING

50

AMAR CHITRA KATHA

YEARS

It was in 1967 that the first Amar Chitra Katha comic rolled off the presses, changing story-telling for children across India forever.

Five decades and more than 400 books later, we are still sharing stories from India's rich heritage, primarily because of the love and support shown by readers like yourself.

SO, FROM US TO YOU, HERE'S A BIG

THANK YOU!

MAHATMA GANDHI

THE EARLY DAYS

www.amarchitrakatha.com

The route to your roots

MAHATMA GANDHI

For Indians, he became Bapu, the father of the nation. To the rest of the world he was a unique general who warred against injustice and hypocrisy in every form. His weapons were truth and non-violence. Family values may have shaped him, but it was his own courage and persistence that made Mohandas Karamchand Gandhi change the way people thought. And that is how he changed the way people lived – for the better.

Script	Illustrations	Editor
Gayatri Madan Dutt	Souren Roy	Anant Pai

Revised By: Prof. C.N. Patel

Cover illustration by: Ramesh Umrotkar

MAHATMA GANDHI — *The early days*

PORBANDAR, GUJARAT — ITS BEACHES CARESSED BY THE WAVES OF THE ARABIAN SEA.

IT WAS ABOUT THE 1820s. KHIMOJI, RANA OF PORBANDAR, WAS TALKING TO HIS PRIME MINISTER.

SURELY, UTTAMCHAND, THERE IS NO DIWAN AS CAPABLE AS YOU.

YOU ARE BEING KIND, RANAJI.

THE PRAISE WAS WELL DESERVED, FOR UTTAMCHAND SERVED HIS RULER DEVOTEDLY.

BUT, AFTER THE RANA'S DEATH, UTTAMCHAND DID NOT RECEIVE THE SAME TREATMENT FROM THE SUCCESSOR, AND HE FELT UNHAPPY.

LAKSHMI, WE CAN NO LONGER STAY HERE. LET US GO TO OUR ANCESTRAL HOME AT KUTIYANA*.

LATER, INVITED BY THE NAWAB OF JUNAGADH, UTTAMCHAND WENT TO HIS COURT TO PAY HIS RESPECTS. HE SALUTED THE NAWAB WITH HIS LEFT HAND.

UTTAMCHAND, WHY THIS DISCOURTESY TO THE NAWAB SAHEB?

SIRE, MY RIGHT HAND IS ALREADY PLEDGED TO PORBANDAR.

BRAVO, UTTAMCHAND. I WOULD GIVE HALF MY KINGDOM TO HAVE A DIWAN LIKE YOU.

THANK YOU, SIRE, BUT I HAVE NO WISH TO SERVE ANY MORE.

SUCH WAS THE TRUTHFULNESS, SENSE OF LOYALTY AND COURAGE OF UTTAMCHAND. HE WAS THE GRANDFATHER OF MOHANDAS GANDHI.

* IN JUNAGADH STATE

1

RAJKOT. THE 1870s. THAKORE BAVAJIRAJ WAS ENJOYING HIMSELF.

THIS IS FINE WINE. THE FINEST I'VE TASTED! HA, HA, HA!

JUST THEN—

THAKORE SAHIB! YOUR DIWAN IS HERE TO SEE YOU.

OH, NO! QUICK, TAKE AWAY THESE GLASSES.

YOU, THERE! OPEN THE WINDOWS. LET THE SMELLS ESCAPE...

THAKORE SAHIB!

HE, HE, HE. COME IN, KARAMCHAND. I WAS... ER... GOING THROUGH THESE IMPORTANT PAPERS...

HMM!... HOW OFTEN I HAVE TOLD YOU THIS. DO NOT LIVE A WASTEFUL LIFE.

WASTEFUL LIFE? ME? OH, REALLY, KARAMCHAND...!

IF A RULER COULD BE IN SUCH AWE OF HIS MINISTER, WHAT KIND OF MAN WAS THIS MINISTER? THE SOUL OF HONESTY! HE WAS THE FATHER OF MOHANDAS GANDHI.

MOHANDAS KARAMCHAND GANDHI WAS BORN IN A THREE-STOREY HOUSE ON THE OUTSKIRTS OF PORBANDAR. KARAMCHAND WAS DIWAN OF PORBANDAR FOR MANY YEARS, AND LATER HE WENT OVER TO RAJKOT. MOHAN'S MOTHER WAS PUTALIBA.

BA, WHY DO YOU FAST SO OFTEN?

FOR YOUR WELFARE. I AM SURE THAT MY PRAYERS AND FASTING WILL BESTOW GOD'S BLESSINGS ON MY FAMILY.

ONE RAINY SEASON—

BA. THE SUN'S COME OUT. YOU MAY BREAK YOUR FAST NOW.

I'M COMING. I MYSELF MUST SEE THE SUN. THAT IS MY VOW.

OH, NO! NOW IT'S GONE BEHIND THE CLOUDS.

NEVER MIND. GOD DOES NOT WANT ME TO EAT TODAY.

AND PUTALIBA CHEERFULLY CONTINUED TO FAST.

MOHAN AND HIS BROTHER, KARSAN, LOVED TO ROAM ABOUT IN THE NEIGHBOURHOOD AND CLIMB UP TREES.

OH... BROTHER, LET GO OF MY LEG... LET GO...

BUMP

AAAH! BA!

* MOTHER

3

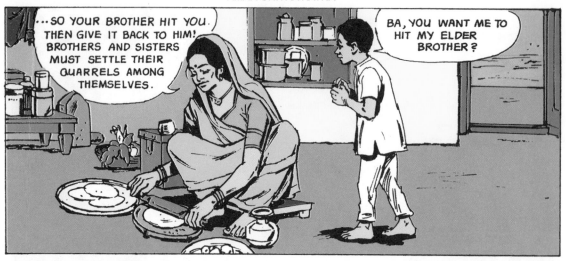

MOHAN ADORED HIS PARENTS AND HIS LOVE FOR THEM WAS FURTHER STRENGTHENED BY THE STORIES HE HEARD FROM THE ANCIENT EPICS.

* THE KING WHO SOLD HIMSELF, HIS WIFE AND SON INTO SLAVERY FOR THE SAKE OF TRUTH.

YET, MOHAN SAW MANY FLAWS IN THE OTHERWISE RICH TRADITION THAT SURROUNDED HIM.

MONIYA, I JUST NOW SAW YOU TOUCHING UKA. HOW COULD YOU? HE CLEANS OUR LATRINES.

BUT, BA, WHAT'S THE DIFFERENCE BETWEEN UKA AND ME? IF GOD IS IN ALL THE WATER AND IN ALL THE LAND,⊕ HE IS IN UKA TOO...

...AN ANSWER THAT MUST HAVE GREATLY SURPRISED PUTALIBA.

MOHAN'S KIND AND GENTLE NATURE MADE HIM HIS MOTHER'S PET, BUT SHE WAS STRICT WITH HIM ABOUT CERTAIN THINGS.

MONIYA, IT'S TIME FOR SCHOOL. HURRY!

I'M COMING, BA.

BUT FOOD IS NOT READY YET.

NEVER MIND, RAMBHA. GIVE ME MY USUAL CURDS, KHAKHRA# AND... UM... SWEET AND SOUR MANGO PICKLE...

MANU, WHAT IS THIS? YOU MUST EAT PROPER MEALS.

I'LL BE LATE, BAPU.

TAKE THE HORSE AND CARRIAGE, THEN.

I'D RATHER WALK! THESE ARE MY HORSE AND CARRIAGE.

SOON AFTER, MOHAN JOINED THE ALFRED HIGH SCHOOL AT RAJKOT WHERE KARAMCHAND HAD TAKEN UP THE POST OF DIWAN.

BOYS, THE EDUCATION INSPECTOR, MR. GILES, IS COMING TODAY. BE SURE TO MAKE A GOOD IMPRESSION.

THE INSPECTOR GAVE THE BOYS FIVE WORDS AS A SPELLING EXERCISE. WHEN THE TEACHER STOPPED TO LOOK OVER MOHAN'S SHOULDER —

?

MOHAN HAD SPELT THE WORD 'KETTLE' WRONG.

⊕ 'JALE VISHNUH, STHALE VISHNUH'— A VERSE FROM THE VISHNU POOJA, OFTEN CHANTED IN THE GANDHI HOUSEHOLD. # UNLEAVENED BREAD ROUNDS BAKED CRISP.

THE TEACHER NUDGED MOHAN'S HEEL WITH THE POINT OF HIS BOOT TO DRAW HIS ATTENTION TO THE SPELLING MISTAKE.

BUT HONEST MOHAN DIDN'T UNDERSTAND THE HINT.

LATER—

MOHANDAS, YOU ARE THE ONLY BOY WHO SPELT A WORD WRONG. AND I SIGNALLED TO YOU TO... WELL, I DON'T UNDERSTAND YOUR STUPIDITY!

BY THIS 'STUPIDITY' A 12-YEAR-OLD WAS ALREADY READYING HIMSELF FOR A GREAT FUTURE IDEAL.

A DREAM TOO WAS FORMING IN THE BOY. WHEN KARAMCHAND ATTENDED THE STATE DURBARS HE HAD TO PUT ON OUTLANDISH STOCKINGS AND BOOTS.

OH, GOD! HOW I HATE THESE... HOW I HATE TO WEAR THEM!

THE BRITISH WANT TO BREAK OUR PRIDE BY SENSELESSLY MAKING US WEAR THEIR KIND OF CLOTHES. WE MUST FREE INDIA OF THEM.

AND AT MOHAN'S SCHOOL, HIS CLASSMATES OFTEN CHANTED A POEM.

THE ENGLISH RULE AND THE INDIANS MEEKLY SUBMIT... FOR LOOK AT THE DIFFERENCE IN THEIR BODILY STRENGTH, THE ENGLISHMAN IS FULL FIVE CUBITS TALL AND IS A MATCH FOR FIVE HUNDRED INDIANS.

IF ALL INDIANS ATE MEAT LIKE THE ENGLISH, MOHAN, WE'D BE ABLE TO CHASE OUT THE ENGLISH.

IS THAT TRUE ? YES, MEHTAB IS RIGHT. HE'S SO STRONG. AND HE ISN'T AFRAID OF GHOSTS, THIEVES AND DARKNESS LIKE ME.

THE SHY, TIMID MOHAN...

...WAS MARRIED AT THIRTEEN TO KASTURBA, ALSO THIRTEEN YEARS OLD. BUT HE HAD NO INTENTION OF BEING A TIMID HUSBAND !

I FORBID YOU TO GO OUT TODAY.

WELL, I WILL GO! DON'T YOU GO OFF SOME-WHERE EVERY EVENING WHEN I TELL YOU NOT TO ? THEN WHY SHOULD I OBEY YOU ?

COME BACK THIS MINUTE, OR I WON'T SPEAK TO YOU AGAIN.

THE TWO QUARRELLED OFTEN. THEY WERE JUST 'MARRIED CHILDREN'!

AND KASTURBA WAS RIGHT IN HER SUSPICIONS ABOUT MOHAN'S MYSTERIOUS EVENING OUTINGS. MOHAN WAS TRYING TO BECOME EQUAL WITH THE BRITISH IN PHYSICAL STRENGTH.

GO ON. EAT IT, MANU.

YES, I WILL EAT MEAT AS A DUTY TO MY COUNTRY.

THAT NIGHT —

OHH !... A GOAT ! A GOAT'S BLEATING IN MY STOMACH !

BUT MOHAN STUCK TO HIS 'DUTY' FOR A YEAR, TILL —

MONIYA, YOU HAVEN'T TOUCHED YOUR DINNER AGAIN TODAY. DID YOU EAT SOMETHING IN BETWEEN?

YES... I MEAN, NO. I...I JUST DON'T FEEL LIKE EATING.

I CAN'T BEAR IT ANYMORE— THIS PRETENDING, THIS LYING TO BA. I WILL NOT EAT MEAT WHILE BA AND BAPU ARE ALIVE.

ABOUT THIS TIME, MOHAN'S ELDER BROTHER GOT INTO DEBT. TO REPAY IT, THE TWO CLIPPED A BIT OF GOLD FROM HIS ARMLET.

THAT EVENING, THEIR PARENTS NOTICED IT. THERE WERE QUESTIONS.

I DON'T KNOW EITHER.

I...I... THE PIECE FELL OFF... I DON'T KNOW WHERE ...

THE THEFT AND THE LIE LAY LIKE A DOUBLE WEIGHT ON MOHAN.

I CANNOT CARRY THIS GUILT WITHIN ME ALL MY LIFE. I CANNOT.

HE WROTE DOWN HIS CONFESSION ON A PIECE OF PAPER AND GAVE IT TO HIS FATHER WHO LAY ILL.

SO BAPU, YOUR SON IS NOW, IN YOUR EYES, NO BETTER THAN A COMMON THIEF ....

KARAMCHAND TORE UP THE PAPER AND LAY DOWN AGAIN. HE ONLY WEPT SILENTLY.

OH, BAPU, YOUR SILENT TEARS WOUND ME MORE THAN A SLAP MIGHT HAVE... THANK YOU, BAPU THANK YOU.

MOHAN SAW THAT LOVE COULD PUNISH MORE EFFECTIVELY THAN VIOLENCE, AND THAT IT PURIFIED THE PERSON PUNISHED. IT WAS AN OBJECT LESSON IN AHIMSA.

THIS LESSON IN AHIMSA BECAME A MORAL IDEAL FOR MOHAN WHEN HE READ THE FOLLOWING VERSES BY THE GUJARATI POET, SHAMAL BHATT:

FOR A BOWL OF WATER, GIVE IN RETURN A GOODLY MEAL. A GOOD TURN DESERVES ONE TEN TIMES AS GOOD WITH ALL ONE'S HEART. THEY WHO RETURN GOOD FOR EVIL; THEY HAVE TRULY WON THE BATTLE FOR LIFE.

FOLLOWING THE IDEAL, MOHAN INDEED WON THE BATTLE OF LIFE AND BECAME ONE OF THE GREATEST OF MEN IN THE HISTORY OF THE WORLD.

OFTEN, MEMBERS OF MOHAN'S FAMILY AND VISITORS OF VARIOUS FAITHS WOULD GATHER ROUND TO DISCUSS THEIR DIFFERENT POINTS OF VIEW WITH KARAMCHAND. MOHAN LISTENED TO THEM KEENLY.

THESE DISCUSSIONS HELPED MOHAN TO DEVELOP EQUAL RESPECT FOR ALL RELIGIONS.

THE ONE PRINCIPLE COMMON TO ALL RELIGIONS WAS TRUTH WITH WHICH MOHAN HAD FALLEN IN LOVE AS A CHILD.

I MUST KNOW THE TRUTH, AND ALWAYS LIVE BY IT.

MOHAN'S FAITH IN TRUTH GREW STRONGER FROM YEAR TO YEAR. MANY YEARS LATER HE WAS TO SAY, "TRUTH IS GOD. IT IS A GOD ANYONE CAN WORSHIP, EVEN AN ATHEIST".

KARAMCHAND, AILING FOR A LONG TIME, DIED IN 1885. PLANS HAD TO BE MADE FOR HIS SONS. IT WAS DECIDED THAT MOHAN SHOULD GO TO ENGLAND AND PREPARE FOR A CAREER IN LAW.

BA, DON'T LOOK SO SAD. BEFORE BOTH BECHARJI MAHARAJ AND YOU, I TAKE THIS VOW: I WILL NOT TOUCH WINE, WOMEN OR MEAT.

DON'T GO...

I MUST, DEAR, FOR OUR FUTURE.

IN BOMBAY, MOHAN'S COMMUNITY THREATENED HIM WITH EXCOMMUNICATION IF HE 'CROSSED THE WATERS'. BUT HE HAD SET HIS HEART ON GOING, AND HE WENT.

IN ENGLAND, EVERYTHING APPEARED STRANGE AND FASCINATING TO MOHAN. IN THE HOTEL LIFT—

IS THIS A ROOM WHERE WE SIT FOR SOME TIME BEFORE WE ARE TAKEN TO OUR ROOMS?

HE JOINED THE INNER TEMPLE OF THE INNS OF COURT IN LONDON.

MOHAN DID NOT BREAK THE VOW HE HAD MADE BEFORE HIS MOTHER.

GANDHI, IN THIS COLD CLIMATE, EITHER YOU TAKE MEAT OR WINE, OR IT IS DEATH.

MY VOW IS SUCH THAT I WILL HAVE TO OPT FOR DEATH!

HE READ A BOOK WHICH MADE HIM A VEGETARIAN BY CHOICE, WHEREAS BEFORE HE HAD BEEN ONE BY BIRTH AND FOR HIS PARENT'S SAKE. HE JOINED THE LONDON VEGETARIAN SOCIETY AND BEGAN TO RELISH BLAND VEGETARIAN FOOD.

HOW GOOD THIS PLAIN BOILED SPINACH TASTES. IT IS TRUE; THE SEAT OF TASTE LIES NOT IN THE TONGUE, BUT IN THE MIND.

THUS BEGAN GANDHI'S LIFE-LONG INTEREST IN DISCOVERING THE RELATION OF FOOD WITH THE HEALTH OF BODY, MIND AND SOUL.

FORGETTING HIS SCHOOL-DAY DISLIKE OF THE ENGLISH IN INDIA, GANDHI ADMIRED THE ENGLISH IN ENGLAND AND TRIED TO MAKE HIMSELF AN ENGLISH GENTLEMAN.

I'VE BEEN TRYING FOR TWENTY MINUTES. THIS TIE JUST WON'T GET ITSELF TIED!

HE TOOK DANCING AND VIOLIN LESSONS, AND JOINED ELOCUTION CLASSES.

THEN ONE DAY, HE SUDDENLY AWOKE FROM THE FALSE DREAM AND DECIDED TO REMAIN INDIAN AND CONCENTRATE ON HIS STUDIES.

A LITTLE LATER, TWO ENGLISH THEOSOPHIST FRIENDS INTRODUCED GANDHI TO TWO OF SIR EDWIN ARNOLD'S BOOKS....

THE SONG CELESTIAL

A translation of the Bhagavad Geeta in English verse

THE LIGHT OF ASIA

A poem on the life of Buddha

...AND A CHRISTIAN ACQUAINTANCE GAVE HIM THE BIBLE TO READ. "THE SERMON ON THE MOUNT" APPEALED TO GANDHI GREATLY.

ALL THREE BOOKS TEACH THE SAME TRUTH THAT RENUNCIATION IS THE HIGHEST FORM OF RELIGION.

GANDHI, EVEN WHILE BEING INDIAN, NOW BECAME A CITIZEN OF BOTH, THE EAST AND THE WEST.

THEN IN 1891, HE RETURNED TO INDIA, A FULL-FLEDGED BARRISTER. AFTER HE LANDED IN BOMBAY—

MANU, BA IS DEAD. BUT SHE DIED KNOWING THAT YOU HAVE PASSED.

BA... MY BELOVED BA.

GANDHI CONTROLLED HIS GRIEF. LIFE HAD TO GO ON.

HE SET UP PRACTICE. BUT HIS SHYNESS HAD NOT LEFT HIM, AND IN A LAW COURT IN BOMBAY, ONE DAY—

SPEAK UP! ... WHY MR. GANDHI, YOU CANNOT UTTER A WORD! WHAT KIND OF A BARRISTER WILL YOU MAKE?

FOR ALMOST TWO YEARS, GANDHI GOT NO WORK. THEN IN 1893, THERE CAME AN OFFER FROM SOME MERCHANTS OF PORBANDAR TO GO TO SOUTH AFRICA AS THEIR LAWYER. GANDHI SEIZED THE OPPORTUNITY AND SET SAIL. SOON —

DURBAN, NATAL. HOW BEAUTIFUL IT LOOKS, LIT UP BY THE SUN.

GANDHI SET FOOT IN THIS COUNTRY OF COALMINES AND SUGAR PLANTATIONS; OF BOUNTIFUL FRUIT AND GRAIN. HIS EMPLOYER, DADA ABDULLA SHETH, WAS THERE TO RECEIVE HIM.

ONE LOOK TOLD GANDHI THE WHOLE STORY. IN THIS RICH LAND, THERE WAS POVERTY — THE POVERTY OF HUMANENESS.

IN THE SECOND WEEK AFTER HIS ARRIVAL, HE TRAVELLED ON WORK TO PRETORIA, CAPITAL CITY OF THE TRANSVAAL. AND HE CAME FACE TO FACE WITH THE INHUMANITY OF SOUTH AFRICA.

HEY, COOLIE! YOU CAN'T SIT HERE. GO TO THE VAN COMPARTMENT.

BUT I HOLD A FIRST CLASS TICKET. THIS IS MY RIGHTFUL SEAT. I WILL NOT GO.

YOU WON'T, EH? WE'LL SEE ABOUT THAT.

GANDHI SAT IN THE DARK WAITING ROOM, NOT ONLY SHIVERING WITH COLD, BUT ALSO TREMBLING WITH HUMILIATION.

SHALL I TAKE THE NEXT SHIP BACK TO INDIA? NO... I WILL STAY, SUFFER THE INSULTS, AND FIGHT THE COLOUR PREJUDICE AGAINST INDIANS.

THE EXPERIENCES CAME THICK AND FAST. IN THE TRANSVAAL, COLOUR PREJUDICE WAS EVEN STRONGER THAN IN NATAL.

SO YOU REFUSE TO SIT AT MY FEET, EH, SAMI *... YOU COOLIE!

AT NIGHT, GANDHI ARRIVED AT JOHANNESBURG. HE WENT TO A HOTEL.

SORRY, NO ROOM.

GRAND NATIONAL HOTEL

IN PRETORIA, HE WAS KICKED FOR WALKING ON THE FOOTPATH IN FRONT OF PRESIDENT KRUGER'S HOUSE.

GANDHI GOT TOGETHER A GROUP OF INDIAN MERCHANTS IN PRETORIA. THEY MET OFTEN TO DISCUSS THEIR PROBLEMS. BUT GANDHI CONCENTRATED FIRST ON FINISHING THE LEGAL WORK HE HAD COME TO DO. HE SOON COMPLETED IT.

I'M GLAD YOU HAVE DECIDED THE CASE OUT OF COURT, ABDULLABHAI. IT'S OVER AND DONE WITH NOW, AND I CAN GO HOME.

TO SHOW MY GRATITUDE, I WOULD LIKE TO ARRANGE A FARE-WELL PARTY FOR YOU.

AND DURING THE PARTY, GANDHI SAW IT!

WHAT! THEY ARE PASSING A LAW THAT WILL TAKE AWAY THE VOTING RIGHTS OF INDIANS?

NATAL MERCURY

Indian Franchise

* CONTEMPTUOUS TERM FOR INDIANS – A CORRUPTION OF "SWAMI"

IT WAS AS IF ALL THE INSULTS HE AND THE INDIAN COMMUNITY SUFFERED STOOD TELESCOPED IN THAT SMALL CORNER OF THE NEWSPAPER.

TAKING AWAY OUR VOTING RIGHTS STRIKES AT THE ROOT OF OUR SELF-RESPECT. YOU MUST FIGHT IT.

GANDHIBHAI, WE ARE UNEDUCATED MEN. WHAT DO WE UNDERSTAND OF THESE MATTERS? BUT IF YOU COULD STAY BACK AND GUIDE US, WE WILL FIGHT.

ALL RIGHT, I WILL DELAY MY DEPARTURE.

AH!... ALLAH IS GREAT AND MERCIFUL.

AND THE PARTY TRANSFORMED ITSELF INTO A PUBLIC COMMITTEE. A POLITE, BUT FIRM PETITION WAS DRAWN UP AND SENT TO THE LEGISLATIVE ASSEMBLY.

AND ON THE THIRD DAY OF THE READING OF THE BILL, FOR THE FIRST TIME, THE LEGISLATIVE ASSEMBLY HALL SAW A STRANGE RUSH OF INDIANS - SUDDENLY CONSCIOUS OF THEIR RIGHTS.

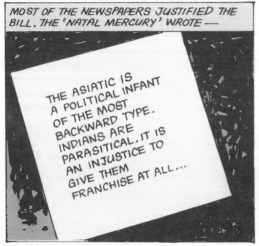

MOST OF THE NEWSPAPERS JUSTIFIED THE BILL. THE 'NATAL MERCURY' WROTE —

THE ASIATIC IS A POLITICAL INFANT OF THE MOST BACKWARD TYPE. INDIANS ARE PARASITICAL. IT IS AN INJUSTICE TO GIVE THEM FRANCHISE AT ALL....

GANDHI REPLIED —

INDIANS COME OF ONE OF THE MOST CIVILISED RACES IN THE WORLD. THEY HAVE EXERCISED THE VOTE LONG BEFORE THE ENGLISH KNEW OF VOTING. NOTHING IS SO WELL ORGANISED AND SO ESSENTIALLY REPRESENTATIVE AS INDIAN VILLAGE COMMUNITY. AND THE INDIANS COMING HERE AS LABOURERS, FAR FROM BEING PARASITICAL, HAVE HELPED TO BUILD NATAL TO PROSPERITY.

THE GOVERNMENT WAS ALARMED. A PROUD INDIAN VOICE HAD RAISED ITSELF. YET THE VOICE SPOKE SO JUSTLY AND WITHOUT AGGRESSIVENESS, THAT SOME PAPERS EVEN PRAISED IT.

NATAL MERCURY WROTE:
WE MUST ADMIT THAT THE INDIANS MAKE OUT A VERY GOOD CASE FROM THEIR POINT OF VIEW.

IN SPITE OF THIS, THE INDIANS, LED BY GANDHI, HAD TO CARRY ON A LONG-DRAWN-OUT STRUGGLE FOR THEIR RIGHTS. IN AUGUST 1894, THE NATAL INDIAN CONGRESS WAS BORN. ENCOURAGED FROM LONDON BY DADABHAI NAOROJI, GANDHI BEGAN HIS 20-YEAR WAR ON SOUTH AFRICAN RACISM.

AND WHEN GANDHI WENT TO INDIA TO BRING BACK HIS FAMILY, HE SPOKE AT MEETINGS TO INTEREST INDIANS IN THE CAUSE OF SOUTH AFRICAN INDIANS.

THEY TREAT US WITH CONTEMPT. SUBMISSION TO THESE INSULTS MEANS DEGRADATION.

GANDHI HAD NOT SAID ANYTHING IN INDIA THAT HE HAD NOT ALREADY SPOKEN OUT LOUD AND CLEAR IN SOUTH AFRICA. YET WHEN HE RETURNED TO DURBAN IN 1897 —

HOW DARE YOU CONDEMN US IN INDIA! TAKE THAT...

...AND THAT!

STOP IT! LEAVE THE POOR MAN ALONE!

THE POLICE SUPERINTENDENT'S WIFE, MRS. ALEXANDER, SHIELDED HIM FROM THE BLOWS.

THE POLICE ARRIVED AND MANAGED TO TAKE HIM TO HIS FRIEND PARSEE RUSTOMJI'S HOUSE, BUT THE CROWD FOLLOWED. SUPERINTENDENT ALEXANDER TRIED TO HUMOUR THE CROWD.

WE'LL HANG OLD GANDHI FROM THE SOUR APPLE TREE...

MEANWHILE, POLICE DETECTIVES, DRESSED AS INDIANS, SECRETLY ESCORTED GANDHI TO THE POLICE STATION.

MR. ESCOMBE, NATAL'S ATTORNEY-GENERAL, CAME TO SEE GANDHI.

YOU ARE BADLY WOUNDED. NAME YOUR ASSAILANTS. I WILL HAVE THEM ARRESTED AND PROSECUTED.

NO, I DON'T WANT TO PROSECUTE ANYONE. THEY ARE NOT TO BLAME. THEIR LEADERS AND A RACIST SOCIETY ARE TO BLAME.

GANDHI CONTINUED HIS NON-AGGRESSIVE POLICY. HE EVEN FORMED AN INDIAN AMBULANCE CORPS DURING THE WAR IN 1899 BETWEEN ENGLAND AND THE BOER* COLONIES OF THE TRANSVAAL TO THE NORTH AND THE ORANGE FREE STATE TO THE WEST OF NATAL.

BY CARRYING THEIR WOUNDED FROM THE FIELD, WE WILL DEMONSTRATE TO THE ENGLISH THAT WE ARE ONE WITH THEM AND SO, ONE OF THEM...

... FOR GANDHI BELIEVED AT THIS TIME THAT THE BRITISH EMPIRE, WITH ALL ITS DEFECTS AND FAULTS, WAS ON THE WHOLE FOR THE GOOD OF MANKIND.

AFTER THE WAR, GANDHI RETURNED TO INDIA IN DECEMBER 1901, AND ATTENDED THE CONGRESS SESSION IN CALCUTTA. HE STAYED WITH GOPAL KRISHNA GOKHALE AND BECAME A CLOSE FRIEND AND FOLLOWER OF HIS.

BEFORE THE YEAR 1902 WAS OUT, GANDHI WAS RECALLED TO SOUTH AFRICA BY HIS INDIAN FRIENDS THERE.

THOUGH THE BOERS WERE DEFEATED BY THE BRITISH, THE PREJUDICE AGAINST INDIANS REMAINED AS STRONG AS BEFORE AND THE BRITISH OFFICIALS, WHO RULED THE CONQUERED COLONIES, ENFORCED OLD LAWS AGAINST THE INDIANS MORE STRICTLY THAN THE FORMER BOER GOVERNMENT.

ON HIS RETURN, GANDHI SETTLED IN THE TRANSVAAL'S PREMIER CITY, JOHANNESBURG. IN HIS HOUSE HERE, LATER, HIS ENGLISH FRIEND HENRY POLAK, HIS SERVANT, AND INDIAN VISITORS, OFTEN LIVED TOGETHER WITH GANDHI'S OWN FAMILY AS MEMBERS OF A LARGE FAMILY.

* THE BOERS WERE THE DESCENDANTS OF DUTCH SETTLERS.

ONE DAY, POLAK GAVE GANDHI A BOOK, "UNTO THIS LAST" BY THE GREAT WRITER, JOHN RUSKIN.

RUSKIN TEACHES THAT THE GOOD OF THE INDIVIDUAL LIES IN THE GOOD OF ALL; THAT A LIFE OF LABOUR AND SIMPLICITY, CLOSE TO NATURE, IS THE LIFE WORTH LIVING.

THE BOOK CAST A MAGIC SPELL ON GANDHI. THE NEXT DAY, HE DECIDED TO PUT RUSKIN'S IDEALS...

...INTO PRACTICE. A FEW KILOMETRES AWAY FROM DURBAN IN NATAL, GANDHI CHOSE A SITE FOR HIS FIRST ASHRAM NAMED PHOENIX AFTER A RAILWAY STATION OF THAT NAME NEAR BY.

IN JUNE 1903, WITH THE HELP OF A FRIEND, GANDHI HAD STARTED A WEEKLY, "INDIAN OPINION" TO CARRY ON HIS FIGHT AGAINST RACIAL LAWS. THE WEEKLY AND THE PRESS WERE REMOVED FROM DURBAN TO THE PHOENIX ASHRAM.

GANDHI'S FAMILY, HIS NEPHEWS, MAGANLAL AND CHHAGANLAL GANDHI, WITH THEIR FAMILIES, THREE ENGLISH FRIENDS AND AN INDIAN WORKER IN THE PRESS, JOINED THE ASHRAM.

THEY BUILT SIMPLE HOUSES FOR THEMSELVES, TILLED THE LAND, AND WORKED FOR "INDIAN OPINION" FOR VERY SMALL PAYMENT.

IN SPITE OF THE INJUSTICES SUFFERED BY THE INDIANS, GANDHI ONCE AGAIN HELPED THE GOVERNMENT IN ITS HOUR OF NEED. WHEN IN 1906, SOME NATIVE AFRICANS CALLED ZULUS WERE PROVOKED INTO REBELLION BY AN UNJUST TAX IMPOSED ON THEM BY THE NATAL GOVERNMENT, GANDHI ORGANISED A STRETCHER BEARER CORPS OF TWENTY-FOUR INDIANS TO REMOVE THE WOUNDED FROM THE BATTLEFIELD. THEIR MAIN DUTY WAS TO NURSE THE WOUNDED ZULUS...

... WHOM THE EUROPEAN VOLUNTEERS AND NURSES REFUSED TO LOOK AFTER. THIS SERVICE PLEASED GANDHI VERY MUCH AND THE INDIANS DID THEIR WORK WITH GREAT CARE AND SYMPATHY.

THIS EXPERIENCE OF HUMANITARIAN SERVICE WAS A TURNING POINT IN GANDHI'S PERSONAL LIFE. AROUND THIS TIME HE REALISED THE NEED FOR SELF-DISCIPLINE.

I WILL HAVE MORE AND MORE OPPORTUNITIES OF RENDERING SUCH SERVICE. I CANNOT DO FULL JUSTICE TO THEM IF AT THE SAME TIME I GO AFTER PLEASURES, HAVE MORE CHILDREN AND THE PROBLEMS OF FAMILY LIFE TO LOOK AFTER.

AND SO, AFTER DISCUSSING THE IDEA WITH KASTURBA, GANDHI TOOK THE VOW OF COMPLETE CELIBACY FOR THE REST OF HIS LIFE. THIS SENSE OF SELF-DISCIPLINE AND SACRIFICE WOULD STAND HIM IN GOOD STEAD FOR THE TASK AHEAD OF HIM.

AS SOON AS THE ZULU REBELLION WAS OVER, THE TRANSVAAL GOVERNMENT REWARDED THE INDIAN COMMUNITY FOR ITS SERVICE WITH A PROPOSAL – WITH A VERY HUMILIATING LAW. IT REQUIRED EVERY INDIAN TO TAKE OUT A REGISTRATION CERTIFICATE, GIVING, LIKE A CRIMINAL, HIS THUMB AND FINGER IMPRESSIONS ON THE APPLICATION. GANDHI CALLED A MEETING OF INDIANS IN JOHANNESBURG'S EMPIRE THEATRE.

LET US TAKE THIS PLEDGE; WE SOLEMNLY DECLARE, WITH GOD AS WITNESS, THAT WE WILL NEVER SUBMIT TO THIS HUMILIATING LAW.

GANDHI WAS THRILLED WITH PRIDE. HE ROSE AND SPOKE.

TO PLEDGE OURSELVES... IN THE NAME OF GOD OR WITH HIM AS WITNESS IS NOT SOMETHING TO BE TRIFLED WITH... EVERYONE MUST BE TRUE TO HIS PLEDGE, EVEN UNTO DEATH, NO MATTER WHAT OTHERS DO. EVEN IF ALL OTHERS GO BACK ON THE PLEDGE AND I AM LEFT ALONE, I WILL DIE, BUT NEVER SUBMIT TO THE LAW.

A THRILL WENT THROUGH EVERY MAN IN THE HALL. THIS WAS THE VOICE OF A GENERAL CALLING HIS TROOPS TO A NEW KIND OF WAR. THEY ROSE TO A MAN.

WITH GOD AS WITNESS, WE PLEDGE THAT WE WILL NEVER SUBMIT TO THIS LAW, AND WILL SUFFER THE PENALTY FOR DISOBEYING IT.

A NEW FORCE IN HUMAN HISTORY WAS BORN ON THIS 11TH DAY OF SEPTEMBER 1906. IN LESS THAN FIFTY YEARS, IT WAS TO FREE INDIA FROM THE IMPERIAL RULE OF BRITAIN, AND THEN, ONE AFTER-ANOTHER, THE OTHER COUNTRIES OF ASIA AND AFRICA HELD IN BONDAGE BY EUROPEAN COLONIAL POWERS.

THIS STRUGGLE WAS CALLED 'PASSIVE RESISTANCE'. BUT GANDHI DID NOT LIKE THE PHRASE. IT DID NOT EXPRESS THE ACTIVE MORAL POWER OF THE NEW WEAPON. HE ADVERTISED A PRIZE FOR ANOTHER SUITABLE NAME.

MY NEPHEW MAGANLAL HAS SUGGESTED IN HIS LETTER THE NAME OF 'SADAGRAHA'- FIRMNESS IN A GOOD CAUSE. AN EXCELLENT NAME; BUT I WILL MAKE A SMALL MODIFICATION.

WE ARE FIGHTING INJUSTICE AND OPPERESSION WITH THE SPIRITUAL WEAPON OF TRUTH. WE WILL THEREFORE CALL IT 'SATYAGRAHA'-FIRMNESS IN FIGHTING INJUSTICE BY SCRUPULOUSLY TRUTHFUL MEANS.

THE NEW LAW WAS PASSED IN MARCH 1907. THE SATYAGRAHA AGAINST IT COMMENCED IN JULY. THE MAJORITY OF INDIANS REFUSED TO APPLY FOR THE CERTIFICATES. LEADING INDIANS, INCLUDING GANDHI, WERE JAILED. BUT NO ONE WEAKENED IN HIS RESOLVE. INDIANS, PREVIOUSLY FRIGHTENED BY THE VERY WORD 'JAIL', HAD, INSPIRED BY GANDHI, LOST ALL FEAR OF IT. THEY CALLED THEIR PRISON "HIS MAJESTY'S HOTEL".

GANDHI WON THIS FIRST BATTLE OF HIS NONVIOLENT FIGHT. GENERAL SMUTS, THE HOME MINISTER, ACCEPTED THE OFFER GANDHI HAD MADE BEFORE STARTING THE SATYAGRAHA...

...THAT THE INDIANS WOULD VOLUNTARILY TAKE OUT THE NEW REGISTRATION CERTIFICATES, AND GIVE THEIR FINGER IMPRESSIONS IF THEY WERE NOT FORCED TO DO SO BY A LAW.

MANY INDIANS DID NOT LIKE THE COMPROMISE. THEY DID NOT UNDERSTAND THE DIFFERENCE BETWEEN VOLUNTARY AND COMPULSORY REGISTRATION. ONE OF THEM, A PATHAN CLIENT OF GANDHI, NAMED MIR ALAM, ASSAULTED GANDHI AS GANDHI WAS GOING TO THE PERMIT OFFICE TO APPLY FOR THE CERTIFICATE.

HEY, RAMA.

BUT THIS TIME ALSO, GANDHI FOLLOWED THE LAW OF AHIMSA. HE WROTE TO THE ATTORNEY GENERAL SAYING THAT HIS ASSAILANTS SHOULD NOT BE PROSECUTED.

THE WOUNDED GANDHI WAS TAKEN BY A NOBLE MISSIONARY, JOSEPH DOKE*, TO HIS HOUSE AND NURSED WITH LOVING CARE. AT GANDHI'S REQUEST HIS LITTLE DAUGHTER, OLIVE, SANG GANDHI'S FAVOURITE ENGLISH HYMN BY CARDINAL NEWMAN.

LEAD, KINDLY LIGHT, AMID THE ENCIRCLING GLOOM, LEAD THOU ME ON...

LIKE SOME INDIANS, MANY EUROPEANS ALSO DID NOT LIKE THE COMPROMISE. UNDER PRESSURE FROM THEM, SMUTS DID NOT REPEAL THE REGISTRATION ACT IN THE MANNER GANDHI AND HIS INDIAN SUPPORTERS WANTED. IN PROTEST, THE INDIANS WHO HAD TAKEN OUT THE VOLUNTARY CERTIFICATES MADE A BONFIRE OF THEM.

* THE NEXT YEAR, IN 1909, HE WROTE GANDHI'S FIRST BIOGRAPHY- "M.K. GANDHI, AN INDIAN PATRIOT IN SOUTH AFRICA"- REPRINTED IN INDIA BY THE PUBLICATIONS DIVISION, GOVERNMENT OF INDIA.

THE SECOND SATYAGRAHA WENT ON FOR THREE YEARS. THE SATYAGRAHI PRISONERS WERE TREATED VERY HARSHLY; MADE TO BREAK STONES, DIG FIELDS AND CLEAN LATRINES.

BUT SATYAGRAHIS' SPIRIT REMAINED UNBROKEN.

EVEN GANDHI WAS NOT SPARED; HE WAS KEPT FOR SOME TIME IN A DARK, NARROW, SOLITARY CELL, AND ASKED TO DO HARD LABOUR.

GANDHI BORE IT ALL WITHOUT ILL-WILL OR ANGER. LATER IN INDIA, HIS PRISONER'S CAP, WITH CHANGES, WOULD BECOME THE NATIONAL KHADI "GANDHI CAP".

WHILE GANDHI WAS IN PRISON, KASTURBA FELL ILL. HE WROTE TO HER FROM JAIL —

I AM VERY MUCH GRIEVED, BUT I AM NOT IN A POSITION TO GO THERE TO NURSE YOU... I CAN COME ONLY IF I PAY THE FINE WHICH I MUST NOT DO... I LOVE YOU SO DEARLY THAT EVEN IF YOU ARE DEAD, YOU WILL BE ALIVE TO ME... IF YOU DIE, YOUR DEATH ALSO WILL BE A SACRIFICE TO THE CAUSE OF SATYAGRAHA.

GANDHI WAS LATER RELEASED, THOUGH THE SATYAGRAHA CONTINUED. GANDHI STARTED ANOTHER ASHRAM IN THE TRANSVAAL CALLED TOLSTOY FARM, ON A LARGE PIECE OF LAND BOUGHT BY A GERMAN FRIEND, HERMAN KALLENBACH. ON THIS FARM, GANDHI WITH HIS WHOLE FAMILY AND THE FAMILIES OF SATYAGRAHIS IN JAIL LIVED A VERY SIMPLE LIFE OF FEW NEEDS AND LABOUR FOR ALL, ACCORDING TO THE IDEALS OF THE GREAT RUSSIAN WRITER, LEO TOLSTOY.

LATER IN LIFE, GANDHI REMEMBERED THE TWO AND A HALF YEARS ON TOLSTOY FARM, WITH ITS DISCIPLINE OF DAILY LABOUR, AS THE HAPPIEST PERIOD IN HIS LIFE. OUT OF THIS EXPERIENCE, GREW GANDHI'S FAMOUS SATYAGRAHA ASHRAM IN AHMEDABAD.

THE SECOND SATYAGRAHA HAD BEEN SUSPENDED IN MAY 1911, WHEN GENERAL SMUTS ASSURED GANDHI THAT THE GOVERNMENT WOULD MEET THE DEMANDS OF THE INDIANS. BUT GENERAL SMUTS DID NOT KEEP THE ASSURANCE HE HAD GIVEN TO GANDHI, AND THE THIRD AND LAST SATYAGRAHA IN SOUTH AFRICA STARTED IN SEPTEMBER 1913. THIS TIME, WOMEN SINGING DEVOTIONAL SONGS ALSO JOINED THE SATYAGRAHA...

LET NOT THY MIND BE AFFECTED BY JOY OR SORROW...

... WITH KASTURBA HERSELF GOING TO JAIL.

DURING THIS SATYAGRAHA, GANDHI HAD INCLUDED A NEW DEMAND THAT THE HEAVY, UNJUST TAX OF THREE POUNDS PER YEAR, WHICH INDENTURED LABOURERS SETTLED IN NATAL HAD TO PAY, SHOULD BE REMOVED. SO THE LABOURERS IN THE COAL-MINES ALSO JOINED THE STRUGGLE. THEY STRUCK WORK AND LEFT THE MINES WITH THEIR FAMILIES AND BELONGINGS. GANDHI LED THEM ALL, MORE THAN TWO THOUSAND IN NUMBER, IN A PEACEFUL MARCH FROM NATAL TO TRANSVAAL, WHICH INDIANS OUTSIDE COULD NOT ENTER.

GANDHI WAS ARRESTED.

AFTER GANDHI'S ARREST, THE GOVERNMENT TRIED TO BREAK THE STRIKE. THE LABOURERS WERE FLOGGED, SHOT AT, AND ASSAULTED BY MOUNTED POLICE.

THERE WAS AN OUTCRY IN INDIA. GOPAL KRISHNA GOKHALE AROUSED STRONG PUBLIC OPINION IN SUPPORT OF THE SATYA-GRAHIS AND EVEN THE VICEROY, LORD HARDINGE, PUBLICLY CONDEMNED THE REPRESSION.

WHEN GANDHI, AFTER HIS RELEASE, HEARD OF THE SUFFERINGS OF THE LABOURERS, HE DISCARDED HIS USUAL DRESS AND FOR SOME TIME ADOPTED A MOURNING DRESS OF A LOINCLOTH AND KURTA, AND SHAVED HIS HEAD.

AT LAST, THE GOVERNMENT YIELDED TO THE MORAL POWER OF SATYAGRAHA AND A FRIENDLY SMUTS CONCEDED ALL THE DEMANDS OF GANDHI IN A GENEROUS SPIRIT.

GREAT WAS THE REJOICING AMONG THE INDIANS. HIS WORK COMPLETE, GANDHI SAILED FOR INDIA VIA ENGLAND. BUT HE LEFT BEHIND A GIFT FOR GENERAL SMUTS-A PAIR OF SANDALS HE HAD MADE HIMSELF. YEARS LATER, SMUTS WAS TO SAY—

I AM NOT WORTHY TO STAND IN THE SHOES OF SO GREAT A MAN.

BUT WHILE IN SOUTH AFRICA, ONE POINT MADE BY A NEWSPAPER WRITER HAD BURST ON GANDHI LIKE A SHOCK WAVE. TRUE, SOUTH AFRICA CAST CONTEMPT ON THE PEOPLE FROM INDIA ...

...INDIA...THE CRADLE OF CIVILIZATION...BUT THE BULK OF THE INDIAN LABOURING CLASS IN SOUTH AFRICA... BEING MOSTLY LOWCASTE, ARE CONDEMNED TO BE A SERVILE RACE BY THE CASTE SYSTEM OF THE HINDOOS. SO THE EVIL FROM WHICH THEY SUFFER IS NOT FROM WITHOUT, BUT FROM WITHIN. IF THEN MR. GANDHI'S FELLOW COUNTRYMEN HAVE CONDEMNED THEMSELVES...TO A MENIAL LOT, HOW CAN HE EXPECT US TO HELP THEM?... HE HAD BETTER BEGIN HIS WORK AT HOME.

OH, GOD! THIS MAN'S ARROW HAS STRUCK MY HEART. YES, WE INDIANS HAVE OURSELVES BUILT OUR OWN PRISON WALLS.

BUT GANDHI WAS GOING HOME NOW. THERE HE MUST BEGIN HIS WORK.

ON JANUARY 9, 1915, A NEW GANDHI DISEMBARKED AT BOMBAY'S APOLLO BUNDAR. INWARDLY, HE ALREADY DEEPLY FELT HIMSELF AN INDIAN; EVEN OUTWARDLY NOW, HE BECAME INDIAN.

GOPAL KRISHNA GOKHALE, GANDHI'S "POLITICAL GUIDE" WAS IN BOMBAY ON THAT DAY. GANDHI CALLED ON HIM.

INDIA IS UNKNOWN TO YOU AND YOU TO HER. TRAVEL ACROSS HER LENGTH AND BREADTH TO GET TO KNOW HER. EXPRESS NO OPINION ON POLITICAL MATTERS FOR A YEAR.

SO FOR THE FIRST YEAR, GANDHI, WITH KASTURBA, TRAVELLED WIDELY THROUGH THE COUNTRY. HE SAW AND LIKED THE PEOPLE'S SIMPLICITY OF NATURE AND LIVING HABITS.

BUT HE ALSO SAW THEIR IGNORANCE AND THEIR INDIFFERENCE TO CLEANLINESS.

HE SAW THE FEAR AND HATRED OF THE RULERS AMONG EDUCATED YOUTH.

ABOVE ALL, HE SAW THE POVERTY OF THE MASSES.

WHILE TOURING, GANDHI SET UP IN MAY 1915, AN ASHRAM AT KOCHARAB, A VILLAGE ON THE OUTSKIRTS OF AHMEDABAD ON THE WESTERN BANK OF THE RIVER SABARMATI. HE NAMED IT "SATYAGRAHA ASHRAM". THE SENIOR MEMBERS OF THE ASHRAM DEDICATED THEMSELVES TO THE SERVICE OF THE COUNTRY AND TOOK EIGHT VOWS TO MAKE THEMSELVES FIT FOR IT.

I SHALL STAND FIRMLY BY TRUTH, AHIMSA, BRAHMACHARYA, CONTROL OF THE PALATE, NON-STEALING, NON-POSSESSION, SWADESHI AND FEARLESSNESS, AND STAND AGAINST UNTOUCHABILITY.

ALSO, THE CONSTITUTION OF THE ASHRAM MADE PHYSICAL LABOUR CUMPULSORY FOR ALL, "AS A DUTY IMPOSED BY NATURE UPON MANKIND."

AS SOON AS HIS YEAR OF POLITICAL SILENCE WAS OVER, GANDHI WENT TO WORK. THE OCCASION: THE CELEBRATIONS IN FEBRUARY 1916, OF THE BANARAS HINDU UNIVERSITY FOUNDED BY PANDIT MADAN MOHAN MALAVIYA WITH THE HELP OF THE BRITISH THEOSOPHIST, MRS. ANNIE BESANT, WHO HAD ADOPTED INDIA AS HER MOTHERLAND.

BANARAS HINDU UNIVERSITY 1916

INVITED TO ADDRESS THE STUDENTS, GANDHI POURED OUT HIS HEART IN A PASSIONATE SPEECH ON WHAT HE HAD SEEN DURING HIS ONE YEAR'S TRAVELS.

I VISITED THE VISHWANATH TEMPLE IN KASHI* LAST EVENING... IS IT RIGHT THAT THE LANES OF OUR SACRED TEMPLE SHOULD BE AS DIRTY AS THEY ARE? ... PEOPLE WALK ABOUT THE STREETS OF BOMBAY UNDER THE PERPETUAL FEAR OF DWELLERS IN THE MULTI-STOREYED BUILDINGS SPITTING UPON THEM ...

AND HE SPOKE OF THE EXTREMES OF LUXURY AND POVERTY IN THE COUNTRY.

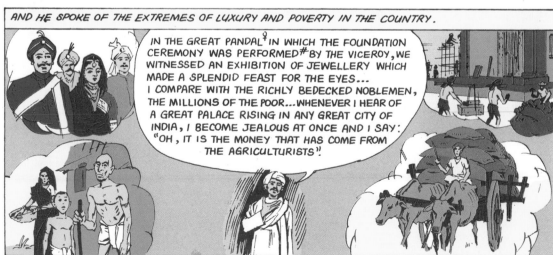

IN THE GREAT PANDAL? IN WHICH THE FOUNDATION CEREMONY WAS PERFORMED# BY THE VICEROY, WE WITNESSED AN EXHIBITION OF JEWELLERY WHICH MADE A SPLENDID FEAST FOR THE EYES... I COMPARE WITH THE RICHLY BEDECKED NOBLEMEN, THE MILLIONS OF THE POOR...WHENEVER I HEAR OF A GREAT PALACE RISING IN ANY GREAT CITY OF INDIA, I BECOME JEALOUS AT ONCE AND I SAY: "OH, IT IS THE MONEY THAT HAS COME FROM THE AGRICULTURISTS".

* VARANASI ? A LARGE PAVILLION SET FOR A PUBLIC FUNCTION.
# ON FEBRUARY 4TH.

AND FINALLY, HE SPOKE OF THE ANARCHIST MOVEMENT SPREADING AMONG THE EDUCATED YOUTH IN THE COUNTRY.

I WOULD SAY TO THEM THAT THEIR ANARCHISM HAS NO ROOM IN INDIA IF INDIA IS TO CONQUER THE CONQUEROR. IT IS A SIGN OF FEAR... I HONOUR THE ANARCHIST FOR HIS BRAVERY IN BEING WILLING TO DIE FOR HIS COUNTRY: BUT I ASK HIM: IS KILLING HONOURABLE?

MRS. BESANT AND THE MAHARAJAS ON THE DAIS DID NOT LIKE GANDHI TALKING SO BOLDLY ABOUT ANARCHISM TO STUDENTS. THEY STOOD UP AND LEFT THE MEETING.

GANDHI ENDED HIS SPEECH ABRUPTLY AND THE MEETING BROKE UP IN CONFUSSION.

INDIA HEARD THIS FEARLESS VOICE AND KNEW THAT SOMEONE DIFFERENT HAD ENTERED THE SCENE. THE POET RABINDRANATH TAGORE GAVE HIM HIS PROPER NAME — MAHATMA, THE GREAT SOUL. AND THE POOR LOOKED UP TO HIM.

MAHATMAJI, I AM FROM CHAMPARAN DISTRICT, BIHAR. OUR ENGLISH LANDLORDS FORCED US TO GROW INDIGO. NOW THAT SYNTHETIC INDIGO HAS BEEN DISCOVERED THEY FORCE US TO PAY THEM COMPENSATION FOR NOT GROWING IT ANY LONGER. HELP US.

GANDHI WENT TO CHAMPARAN. THE GOVERNMENT ORDERED HIM TO LEAVE, WHICH HE REFUSED TO DO. HE WOULD INSTEAD GO WILLINGLY TO JAIL. THE NEWS SPREAD.

A LAWYER MAHATMA HAS COME, WHO IS GOING TO JAIL FOR OUR SAKE.

HE WANTS NOTHING FROM US; ONLY JUSTICE FOR US FROM THE ENGLISH.

AND THE VILLAGERS GATHERED IN CROWDS ROUND THE COURTHOUSE, STIRRED BY AN ANCIENT INDIAN MEMORY, DEAD NOW FOR CENTURIES, THAT A LEADER MUST BE FATHER TO HIS PEOPLE. HERE HE WAS — BAPU.*

BAPU...

BAPU...

BAPU...

GANDHI SUCCEEDED IN CONFOUNDING BOTH THE MAGISTRATE AND THE PLEADER AND WAS QUICKLY RELEASED. THEN QUIETLY, POLITELY, PAINSTAKINGLY, HE WORKED TO MAKE THE LANDLORDS RETURN PART OF WHAT THEY HAD FORCIBLY TAKEN FROM THE PEASANTS. HE HAD SHOWN THE PEASANTS, COWERING TILL NOW UNDER BRITISH AUTHORITY, THAT THEY NEED FEAR IT NO LONGER. IT WAS HERE THAT HE MET RAJENDRA PRASAD AND J.B. KRIPALANI.

* FATHER

GANDHI ALSO BEGAN A PROGRAMME OF CLEANLINESS IN CHAMPARAN'S VILLAGES, SWEEPING, CLEARING, TEACHING THE VILLAGERS THAT THERE IS DIGNITY IN CLEANING UP OUR OWN DIRT.

CHAMPARAN TOO TAUGHT HIM SOMETHING—THAT THE ENGLISH, THOUGH BASICALLY JUST, MUST LEAVE INDIA. FOR IN ORDER TO RULE HER, THEY BROKE HER BACK.

WHILE WORKING IN CHAMPARAN, GANDHI SHIFTED THE SATYAGRAHA ASHRAM FROM KOCHARAB TO ANOTHER SPOT TO THE NORTH, ALSO ON THE WESTERN BANK OF THE SABARMATI, CLOSE TO THE SABARMATI JAIL.

AN IDEAL SITE FOR THE JAIL-LOVING SATYAGRAHI. THE SABARMATI RIVER CONTINUES TO ADD BEAUTY TO IT.

GANDHI HAD BEAUTIFIED HIS ASHRAM EVEN MORE—A FAMILY OF 'UNTOUCHABLES' OR 'HARIJANS' * AS HE ADDRESSED THEM LATER, HAD JOINED THE ASHRAM AT KOCHARAB AND NOW LIVED WITH HIM.

LIFE IN THE ASHRAM FOLLOWED A STRICT DISCIPLINE OF FIXED HOURS OF PRAYER, MORNING AND EVENING. ONE OF THE SANSKRIT VERSES IN THE MORNING PRAYER WAS:

I DO NOT DESIRE EITHER KINGDOM OR HEAVEN OR FREEDOM FROM REBIRTH. I ONLY DESIRE END TO THE SUFFERINGS OF ALL CREATURES.

THE ASHRAM MEMBERS ALSO DID SEVERAL HOURS OF MANUAL LABOUR; BESIDES SPINNING AND WEAVING, SCAVENGING AND CLEANING LATRINES.

THIS WAS GANDHI'S WAY OF TRAINING HIS NON-VIOLENT ARMY OF VOLUNTEERS TO FEEL ONE WITH THE LOWEST CLASS IN SOCIETY.

* LITERALLY PEOPLE OF GOD, THE TERM FIRST USED BY RAMANUJACHARYA AND LATER NARSI MEHTA, BEFORE MAHATMA GANDHI.

GANDHI NEXT TOOK UP THE CAUSE OF AHMEDABAD'S POORLY PAID MILL WORKERS WHO WERE ASKING FOR A RAISE IN WAGES. THEY PLEDGED TO CONTINUE THE STRIKE TILL THE MILL-OWNERS AGREED TO THE RAISE.

THE OWNERS STOOD FIRM. THE WORKERS BEGAN TO TIRE. GANDHI WAS UPSET; THEY MUST NOT GIVE UP NOW. HOW COULD HE CONVINCE THEM?

IT IS TO THEIR GOOD TO STAY UNITED. MY BELOVED BA USED TO FAST FOR OUR GOOD...

AND THE NEXT MOMENT—

FRIENDS, UNDER OUR EK TEK* TREE, I ANNOUNCE THIS: I SHALL NOT TOUCH FOOD BECAUSE YOU ARE NOT UNITED IN YOUR PLEDGE.

BAPU, NO! DO NOT DO THIS; NOT FOR OUR SAKE.

FOR THE FIRST TIME, THROUGH A FAST, THROUGH SELF-DENIAL, A LEADER WAS PLAYING A DEEPLY PERSONAL ROLE, OF PARENT TO HIS CHILDREN.

THIS FAST IS NOT TO BLACKMAIL THE MILL-OWNERS. I HAVE CLEARLY TOLD THEM THAT. IT IS FOR THE WELFARE OF THE WORKERS.

FINALLY, THE MILL-OWNERS RELENTED. IT WAS AS IF THEY HAD BEEN REMINDED THAT IT WAS ONLY A PATERNAL EMPLOYER WHO REALLY SUCCEEDED.

AFTER THIS CAME THE ISSUE OF THE CULTIVATORS OF KHEDA DISTRICT TO THE SOUTH-EAST OF AHMEDABAD. OWING TO EXCESSIVE RAIN DURING THE PREVIOUS MONSOON, THE CROPS HAD FALLEN BELOW THE NORMAL LEVEL.

THE PEOPLE DEMANDED THAT THE COLLECTION OF LAND REVENUE SHOULD BE POSTPONED TO THE NEXT YEAR. BUT THE GOVERNMENT DID NOT AGREE TO THIS.

GANDHI ADVISED THE CULTIVATORS NOT TO PAY THE LAND REVENUE. THE GOVERNMENT CONFISCATED THE CATTLE THE HOUSEHOLD GOODS...

... AND EVEN THE STANDING CROPS IN THE FIELDS OF THOSE WHO DID NOT PAY.

* EK TEK – 'ONE PLEDGE'.

THIS RESULTED IN MUCH SUFFERING AMONG THE FARMERS, TILL, UNDER PRESSURE FROM THE VICEROY, THE GOVERNMENT OF BOMBAY CHANGED ITS POLICY AND THE COLLECTOR OF KHEDA INFORMED GANDHI THAT THE CULTIVATORS WHO WERE TOO POOR TO PAY WOULD NOT BE FORCED TO DO SO. THE FIGHT WAS THE BEGINNING OF THE EDUCATION OF THE PEOPLE OF GUJARAT IN SATYAGRAHA, A LESSON IN COURAGE AND SELF-SACRIFICE. AND IT GAVE THEM A NEW LEADER, VALLABHBHAI PATEL WHO BECAME GANDHI'S LOYAL LIEUTENANT IN ALL HIS SATYAGRAHA BATTLES.

SOON AFTER THIS, ALTHOUGH LOKAMANYA TILAK WAS AGAINST IT, GANDHI HELPED ENGLAND RECRUIT SOLDIERS FOR WORLD WAR-I. THE MESSAGE WAS CLEAR— DO UNTO US AS WE DO UNTO YOU. INDIA WANTED HOME RULE IN FAIR EXCHANGE FOR HER WAR EFFORTS. BUT, AT THE END OF THE WAR—

THE BRITISH HAVE PASSED THE ROWLATT ACTS TO KILL THE PEOPLE'S SPIRIT OF FREEDOM. THE HARSH WAR-TIME MEASURES ARE TO CONTINUE.

IS THIS OUR REWARD FOR ALL THE BLOOD INDIANS SPILT FOR THEM IN THE WAR?

IN PROTEST, GANDHI TOOK HIS FIRST MAJOR POLITICAL STEP IN INDIA. HE CALLED FOR A NATION-WIDE SATYAGRAHA; A HARTAL. ALL SHOPS, BUSINESS ESTABLISHMENTS, MILLS AND FACTORIES WERE TO BE VOLUNTARILY CLOSED ON SUNDAY, APRIL 6, 1919. THE CALL WAS FOLLOWED THROUGHOUT THE COUNTRY.

A NATION COMING PEACEFULLY TO A HALT WAS QUITE A SPECTACLE.

GANDHI WAS ARRESTED ON APRIL 9. AS A REACTION THERE WAS VIOLENCE IN SOME PLACES— DELHI, AMRITSAR, AHMEDABAD AND VIRAMGAM*. GANDHI WAS DEEPLY PAINED.

WHAT A GREAT BLOT ON SATYAGRAHA! I HAVE MADE A HIMALAYAN MIS-CALCULATION. I BELIEVED WRONGLY THAT THE PEOPLE WOULD KEEP PERFECT PEACE.

HE CALLED OFF THE SATYAGRAHA.

* A TOWN NEAR AHMEDABAD.

THEN CAME APRIL 13, BAISAKHI, AND THE MASSACRE AT JALLIANWALA BAGH IN AMRITSAR. AN ARMY OFFICER, GENERAL DYER, ANGERED BY THE KILLING OF SOME ENGLISHMEN IN THE CITY AND THE ASSAULT ON AN ENGLISHWOMAN ON THE 10TH BY AN EXCITED CROWD, WANTED TO PUNISH THE PEOPLE. UNDER HIS ORDERS SEPOYS FIRED ON AN UNARMED CROWD AND KILLED MORE THAN A THOUSAND*PEOPLE AND WOUNDED MORE THAN THREE THOUSAND.

THE SOLDIERS FIRED 1650 ROUNDS IN TEN MINUTES, AND STOPPED ONLY WHEN THEY HAD NO MORE AMMUNITION.

ON APRIL 15, MARTIAL LAW WAS IMPOSED IN MANY PARTS OF THE PUNJAB. COLLEGE STUDENTS IN LAHORE WERE FORCED TO WALK SEVERAL MILES IN THE HOT SUN TO ATTEND CUMPULSORY ROLL CALL TWICE A DAY.

SOME WERE FLOGGED IN PUBLIC.

AND THE PEOPLE PASSING THROUGH THE STREET IN WHICH THE ENGLISHWOMAN WAS ASSAULTED WERE FORCED TO CRAWL ON THEIR BELLIES.

ONE DISTRICT WAS BOMBED FROM THE AIR.

RESPECTABLE CITIZENS WERE ARRESTED WITHOUT WARRANT AND HANDCUFFED.

THE REIGN OF TERROR LASTED SIX WEEKS. BECAUSE OF THE MARTIAL LAW, FOR MANY DAYS, THE REST OF THE COUNTRY DID NOT KNOW WHAT WAS HAPPENING IN THE PUNJAB. BUT SLOWLY THE HORROR STORIES SPREAD, AND THE PEOPLE WERE SHOCKED.

* THE BRITISH GAVE THE FIGURES AS 379 KILLED AND OVER 1,200 WOUNDED.

GANDHI WAS NOT ALLOWED TO GO TO PUNJAB FOR SEVERAL MONTHS. WHEN AT LAST HE WENT THERE IN OCTOBER, FIRST TO LAHORE AND THEN TO AMRITSAR, LARGE CROWDS WELCOMED HIM.

WRITING IN HIS MAGAZINE, NAVAJIVAN, GANDHI SAID —

PEOPLE WHO HAD SUFFERED MUCH, WASHED AWAY THEIR GRIEF WITH THE WATERS OF LOVE.

BUT SOON, IN DECEMBER 1919, KING GEORGE V MADE AN APPEAL TO THE PEOPLE OF INDIA AND HIS OFFICIALS IN THE GOVERNMENT.

FORGET THE PAST, AND CO-OPERATE IN WORKING THE NEW REFORMS ACT IN THE PROPER SPIRIT

GANDHI TRUSTED THE BRITISH AND WELCOMED THE PROPOSAL.

ON DECEMBER 29, AT THE INDIAN NATIONAL CONGRESS SESSION AT AMRITSAR, PRESIDED OVER BY MOTILAL NEHRU, A NEW SLOGAN BEGAN TO DOMINATE THE POLITICAL HORIZON.

MAHATMA GANDHI KI JAI!

GANDHI WAS ESTABLISHED AND ACKNOWLEDGED AS A LEADER OF THE NATION.

' I do not claim that I have not committed any mistakes, but this I claim that at any given time, I did what I considered right at that time.'

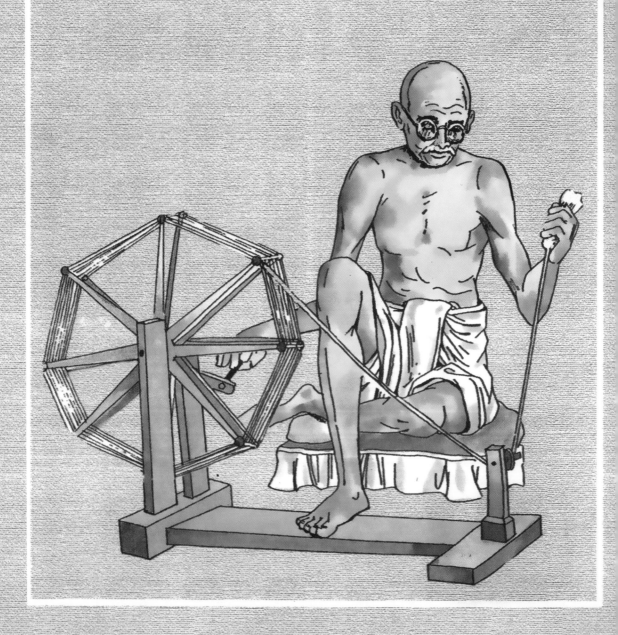

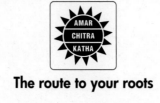

The route to your roots

VEER SAVARKAR

The prison of Kala Pani was the destination for many Indian freedom fighters. Scores of revolutionaries were exiled to this dreaded cellular prison which was in Port Blair in the Andaman Islands. Veer Savarkar was one of them. Hounded by the police from London to Marseilles and then to India, he faced the most trying situations in his untiring effort to fight British rule. But even the despair and darkness of Kala Pani did not dim his courage. Veer Savarkar found the most unique ways to motivate his prison mates and keep their belief alive in an independent India.

Script
Subba Rao

Illustrations
Ram Waeerkar

Editor
Anant Pai

VEER SAVARKAR
IN THE ANDAMANS

1907: AT INDIA HOUSE IN LONDON, THE HEADQUARTERS OF ABHINAV BHARAT...

...FROM WHERE VINAYAK DAMODAR SAVARKAR DIRECTED THE ACTIVITIES OF THE INDIAN REVOLUTIONARIES IN ENGLAND—

HERE IS A LITTLE GIFT FOR YOU, MY FRIEND.

EXCELLENT COVER! NEAT BINDING!

OPEN THE BOOK! YOU'LL LIKE THE CONTENTS EVEN BETTER.

SAVARKAR! WHAT A BRILLIANT IDEA! WELL I...

TAKE IT WITH YOU TO INDIA. BUT REMEMBER...

...IT MUST NOT BE USED TILL WE CONSOLIDATE OUR BASE THERE.

SAVARKAR AND HIS ASSOCIATES WORKED TIRELESSLY TO INFORM THE PEOPLE OF EUROPE OF INDIA'S STRUGGLE FOR FREEDOM AND TO SEEK THEIR SUPPORT.

AH, MADAM CAMA! SO YOU ARE BACK FROM GERMANY. WHAT HAPPENED AT STUTTGART?

DID OUR PLAN WORK? DOES ALL EUROPE KNOW THAT INDIANS WANT FREEDOM AND ARE PREPARED TO DIE FOR IT?

WELL... DELEGATES HAD COME FROM ALL OVER EUROPE TO ATTEND THE SOCIALIST CONGRESS. I UNFURLED THE FLAG AT THE CONFERENCE.

THIS FLAG, THE FLAG OF INDIAN INDEPENDENCE, IS SANCTIFIED BY THE BLOOD OF MARTYRED INDIAN YOUTHS.

I CALL UPON YOU, GENTLEMEN, TO RISE AND SALUTE IT.

AND SAVARKAR, THE WHOLE ASSEMBLY STOOD UP AS ONE MAN!

SAVARKAR'S MAIN MISSION IN ENGLAND WAS TO FIND ARMS AND AMMUNITION FOR HIS COUNTRYMEN IN INDIA.

BAPAT! IT'S GOOD TO SEE YOU BACK. WAS YOUR VISIT TO PARIS FRUITFUL?

VERY! I'VE LEARNT THE ART OF MAKING BOMBS.

I HAVE BROUGHT A GIFT FOR YOU.

BOMB MANUAL

THE ORIGINAL WAS IN RUSSIAN. IT WAS TRANSLATED INTO ENGLISH FOR ME.

THIS IS JUST WHAT WE NEEDED. NOW WE CAN SET UP BOMB FACTORIES IN INDIA.

BAPAT, MAKE SURE THAT THE MANUAL REACHES INDIA SAFELY. AND REMEMBER... WE MUST ESTABLISH A CHAIN OF BOMB FACTORIES THROUGHOUT INDIA BEFORE THE FIRST BOMB IS THROWN.

IN LONDON, SAVARKAR ADDRESSED A NATIONAL CONFERENCE IN SUPPORT OF THE DEMAND FOR SWARAJ.

...BEFORE PASSING THIS RESOLUTION JUST BRING BEFORE YOUR MIND'S EYE THE DREADFUL PRISON WALLS... THE DREARY DINGY CELLS...

THE RESOLUTION WAS PASSED UNANIMOUSLY.

LATER—

SAVARKAR, ONE OF OUR ASSOCIATES IS NOT TO BE TRUSTED.

REALLY? WHO IS THE MAN, AIYAR?

KIRTIKAR, THE DENTAL STUDENT.

WHY DIDN'T YOU TELL ME EARLIER?

THAT NIGHT AIYAR AND SAVARKAR RAIDED KIRTIKAR'S ROOM AT INDIA HOUSE.

LOOK, SAVARKAR! IT'S A REPORT ABOUT US... IT'S FOR THE POLICE. I KNEW HE WAS...

SH...

I HEAR FOOT-STEPS.

IN INDIA, SAVARKAR'S ELDER BROTHER, GANESHRAO, WAS ARRESTED. WHEN THE NEWS REACHED LONDON, MADANLAL DHINGRA—AN ENGINEERING STUDENT WHO WAS ALREADY SEETHING WITH ANGER AT THE TREATMENT METED OUT TO FREEDOM FIGHTERS IN INDIA—CAME TO FIND OUT WHY.

WHAT WAS GANESHRAO'S CRIME, SAVARKAR?

HE PUBLISHED A BOOK OF PATRIOTIC POEMS.

WOULD YOU LIKE TO HEAR ONE OF THEM, MADAN?

I WOULD!

PRAY, TELL, WAS POLITICAL FREEDOM EVER WON WITHOUT A WAR?

HE IS ABSOLUTELY RIGHT.

VIOLENCE SHALL BE MET WITH VIOLENCE. THE OPPRESSION OF MY COUNTRYMEN WILL NOT GO UNAVENGED.

MADANLAL DHINGRA SHOT SIR CURZON WYLLIE, THE ADVISER TO THE GOVERNMENT ON INDIAN AFFAIRS.

DHINGRA DEFENDED HIS ACT. I SHED ENGLISH BLOOD INTENTIONALLY AND ON PURPOSE AS A PROTEST AGAINST THE INHUMAN TRANSPORTATION AND HANGING OF INDIAN YOUTH.

LATER, IN A STATEMENT DHINGRA EXPLAINED —

Just as the Germans have no right to occupy this country, so the English people have no right to occupy India; and it is perfectly justifiable on our part to kill the Englishman who is polluting our sacred land.

EVEN SO, HIS COMPATRIOTS IN LONDON CONDEMNED HIS ACTION.

THIS MEETING UNANIMOUSLY CONDEMNS MADANLAL DHINGRA...

I BEG YOUR PARDON, NOT UNANIMOUSLY.

SAVARKAR WAS MANHANDLED.

PULL HIM DOWN!

DRIVE HIM OUT!

TAKE THIS!

SAVARKAR REFUSED TO CONDEMN DHINGRA. AT THE SAME TIME HE DID NOT APPROVE OF THE CRUDE BEHAVIOUR OF SOME STUDENTS.

YOU SHOULD HAVE SEEN LADY CURZON WYLLIE THROWING HERSELF ON THE BODY OF HER HUSBAND. HA! HA!

STOP IT!

A WIFE SOBS HER HEART OUT FOR HER HUSBAND AND YOU LAUGH AT HER! SHAME ON YOU!

MEANWHILE IN INDIA, JACKSON, THE BRITISH COLLECTOR OF NASIK, WHO HAD TAKEN GANESHRAO SAVARKAR INTO CUSTODY WAS SHOT DEAD.

THE POLICE ARRESTED THE SUSPECTS.

VINAYAK SAVARKAR HIMSELF WAS ARRESTED ON MARCH 13, 1910 AT VICTORIA STATION IN LONDON...

...AND DEPORTED TO INDIA. S.S. MOREA, THE STEAMER CARRYING SAVARKAR, SAILED FROM LONDON ON JULY 1, 1910.

THE SHIP HAD TO DROP ANCHOR OFF THE FRENCH PORT OF MARSEILLES, FOR A COUPLE OF DAYS.

THIS IS A GODSEND!

I'D LIKE TO GO TO THE LAVATORY. MAY I?

I'LL TAKE YOU THERE.

THE GUARD TOOK HIM TO THE LAVATORY.

BE QUICK!

SAVARKAR WAS INDEED VERY QUICK! HE TOOK OFF HIS DRESSING-GOWN, THREW IT OVER THE GLASS PANE OF THE DOOR...

... JUMPED UP TO THE PORTHOLE IN THE LAVATORY...

...AND CAME OUT.

AS HE DIVED, HOWEVER...

...A GUARD ON THE DECK SPOTTED HIM.

THE GUARD OPENED FIRE.

BULLETS WHIZZED PAST, BUT SAVARKAR SWAM ON WITHOUT LOOKING BACK.

WHEN HE REACHED THE HARBOUR OF MARSEILLES...

...AND CLIMBED ONTO THE QUAY—

THIEF! THIEF!

YOU CANNOT TOUCH ME. YOU ARE BRITISH GUARDS. AND I AM ON FRENCH SOIL.

LET'S SEE WHO STOPS US.

SAVARKAR APPEALED TO A FRENCH POLICE-MAN BUT IN VAIN.

THE GUARDS DRAGGED HIM BACK TO THE SHIP. MADAM CAMA AND AIYER HURRIED TO MARSEILLES, BUT THEY WERE TOO LATE TO BE OF ANY HELP.

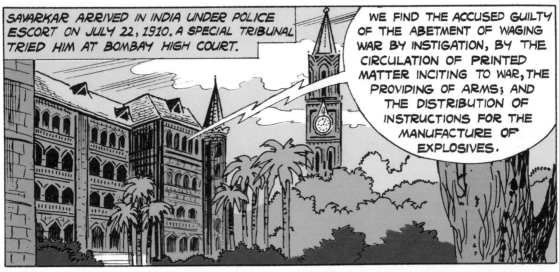

SAVARKAR ARRIVED IN INDIA UNDER POLICE ESCORT ON JULY 22, 1910. A SPECIAL TRIBUNAL TRIED HIM AT BOMBAY HIGH COURT.

WE FIND THE ACCUSED GUILTY OF THE ABETMENT OF WAGING WAR BY INSTIGATION, BY THE CIRCULATION OF PRINTED MATTER INCITING TO WAR, THE PROVIDING OF ARMS; AND THE DISTRIBUTION OF INSTRUCTIONS FOR THE MANUFACTURE OF EXPLOSIVES.

VINAYAK DAMODAR SAVARKAR, THE SENTENCE OF THE COURT UPON YOU IS TRANSPORTATION FOR LIFE AND FORFEITURE OF ALL YOUR PROPERTY.

SAVARKAR WAS ALSO TRIED FOR THE MURDER OF JACKSON, THE COLLECTOR OF NASIK.

THE GUN WITH WHICH JACKSON WAS KILLED WAS THE GUN SAVARKAR HAD DESPATCHED FROM LONDON.

SAVARKAR WAS SENTENCED TO TRANSPORTATION FOR LIFE ON THIS COUNT ALSO — ALTHOUGH HE DECLARED HIS INNOCENCE.

I AM PREPARED TO FACE UNGRUDGINGLY THE EXTREME PENALTY OF YOUR LAWS, IN THE BELIEF THAT IT IS THROUGH SUFFERING AND SACRIFICE ALONE THAT OUR BELOVED MOTHERLAND CAN MARCH ON TO AN ASSURED, IF NOT SPEEDY, TRIUMPH.

SAVARKAR WAS TAKEN TO DONGRI JAIL IN BOMBAY.

SINCE HE WAS ARRESTED ON FRENCH SOIL SEVERAL FRENCH NEWSPAPERS DEMANDED THAT SAVARKAR SHOULD BE RETURNED TO FRANCE. AN INTERNATIONAL TRIBUNAL HEARD THE APPEAL. SAVARKAR WAITED AT DONGRI FOR THE VERDICT.

MR. SAVARKAR, I HAVE BAD NEWS FOR YOU.

THE INTERNATIONAL TRIBUNAL HAS GIVEN ITS JUDGMENT IN FAVOUR OF BRITAIN.

A SENTENCE OF TRANSPORTATION FOR LIFE MEANS TWENTY-FIVE YEARS IN THE ANDAMANS. YOU HAVE TO SERVE TWO SUCH SENTENCES— THAT MEANS FIFTY YEARS IN THE ANDAMANS.

THIS IS THE IRON PLATE YOU HAVE TO WEAR.

IS BRITISH RULE ITSELF GOING TO LAST FOR FIFTY YEARS?

THESE TURNED OUT TO BE THE MOST PROPHETIC WORDS EVER SPOKEN BY A FREEDOM FIGHTER.

LATER, HIS WIFE WAS ALLOWED TO MEET HIM.

DON'T YOU RECOGNISE ME?

ONLY MY DRESS HAS CHANGED. I AM THE SAME.

SAVARKAR WAS TAKEN TO THE BYCULLA JAIL AND LATER TO THE JAIL AT THANE. A FRIENDLY WARDER CALLED ON HIM.

MASTER, YOUR YOUNGER BROTHER IS IN THIS SAME JAIL.

THE YOUNGER BROTHER, NARAYANRAO, HAD BEEN IMPRISONED ON THE CHARGE OF BEING INVOLVED IN AN ATTEMPT ON THE LIFE OF THE VICEROY!

HERE IS A MESSAGE FROM HIM.

SAVARKAR READ THE MESSAGE IN THE DIM LIGHT.

WOULD YOU LIKE TO SEND HIM A REPLY?

YES.

THE FRIENDLY WARDER HELD A LANTERN WHILE SAVARKAR WROTE IN THE DEAD HOURS OF THE NIGHT.

SOME FUEL HAS TO BURN IN A STEAM-ENGINE SO THAT STEAM MAY RISE UP FROM IT AND THE ENGINE BEGIN TO MOVE. ARE WE NOT THAT FUEL?

INMATES BOUND FOR THE ANDAMANS WERE OUT OF THE PRISON.

COME ON, BRETHREN WE ARE PROCEEDING TO THE ANDAMANS.

SAVARKAR WAS TAKEN TO THE STATION IN A CAR.

IS HE A KING? WHY IS HE BEING TAKEN IN A CAR?

EVIDENTLY THE GOVERNMENT IS AFRAID OF HIM.

SAVARKAR HAD SHACKLES ON HIS FEET AND HE WAS CHAINED TO THE OFFICER BY ONE RING OF HIS HANDCUFFS.

I AM SORRY, MY FRIEND. FOR THE TIME BEING YOU HAVE TO BE A PRISONER LIKE ME.

IF YOU REALLY CARE FOR ME, DON'T TRY TO ESCAPE AS YOU DID IN MARSEILLES.

I WON'T.

THE MADRAS-BOUND TRAIN LEFT THANE.

THE TRAIN IS DELIVERING ME TO THE ANDAMANS WITH THE RAPIDITY OF LIGHTNING.

WILL IT TAKE ME BACK HOME WITH THE SAME SPEED?

Cont. on page 18

KALA PANI
(Andaman and Nicobar Islands)

Script: Swarn Khandpur
Illustrations: S.K. Parab

IN THE BAY OF BENGAL LIES A CLUSTER OF ISLANDS KNOWN AS THE BAY ISLANDS.

PORT BLAIR

TEN DEGREE CHANNEL

OVER THREE HUNDRED IN NUMBER, LUSH AND PICTURESQUE, THEY FORM THE ANDAMAN AND NICOBAR ARCHIPEL-AGOS. THE TWO GROUPS OF ISLANDS FORM A SINGLE ADMINISTRATIVE UNIT AS A UNION TERRITORY AND ARE REACHED BY STEAMERS FROM CALCUTTA AND MADRAS. THE GREAT NICOBAR ISLAND IS THE SOUTHERN-MOST TIP OF INDIA.

TILL THE END OF THE 18TH CENTURY, THE ANDAMAN ISLANDS WERE THE EXCLUSIVE HOME OF THE NEGRITOS, AN ANCIENT PYGMY RACE OF THE STONE AGE. IN 1971 THEY NUMBERED LESS THAN 500 AND ARE NOW THREATENED WITH EXTINCTION. STILL IN THE 'HUNTING AND FOOD-GATHERING' STAGE, THEY USE THE BOW FOR BOTH FISHING AND HUNTING.

UNLIKE THE NEGRITOS, THE NICOBARESE ARE OF MONGOLOID STOCK. THEY PRACTISE FARMING AND CONSTRUCT THEIR HUTS ON STILTS IN THE GROVES OF WILD COCONUT PALMS.

ELEPHANTS FROM THE MAINLAND ARE BROUGHT TO THE ISLANDS TO WORK IN THE DENSE, EVER-GREEN FORESTS.

SOLITARY CELL WHERE SAVERKAR 123 WAS FREQUENTLY KEPT *

THE WORLD'S LARGEST TURTLES AND ROBBER CRABS ABOUND IN THE WATERS SURROUNDING THE ISLANDS.

PORT BLAIR, THE MAIN HARBOUR, IS THE CAPITAL OF THE ISLANDS. THE BRITISH USED THE ANDAMANS AS A PENAL COLONY. THEY BUILT THE GHASTLY CELLULAR JAIL WHERE THEY IMPRISONED NOT ONLY CRIMINALS BUT SEVERAL FREEDOM-FIGHTERS AS WELL. THE ARCHIPELAGO WAS ONCE THE MOST DREADED PLACE IN THE COUNTRY AND WAS REFERRED TO AS KALA PANI (BLACK WATERS). SUBHAS CHANDRA BOSE NAMED THE ISLANDS SHAHEED AND SWARAJ — THE ISLANDS WHERE FREEDOM-FIGHTERS HAD BECOME MARTYRS SO THAT THE COUNTRY COULD WIN FREEDOM!

* AS SPELT ON THE WALL OF THE CELL

FROM MADRAS SAVARKAR AND THE OTHER PRISONERS WERE TAKEN TO THE ANDAMANS IN THE SHIP S.S. MAHARAJA.

THE SHIP REACHED PORT BLAIR, THE CAPITAL OF THE ANDAMANS, ON JULY 4, 1911.

WHAT AN IDEAL NAVAL BASE THESE ISLANDS WOULD MAKE IN INDEPENDENT INDIA!

AND TRUE ENOUGH, WE NOW HAVE A NAVAL BASE AT THE ANDAMANS.

AS THEY MARCHED TO THE JAIL NEARBY—

YOU ARE GOING UP THIS SLOPE TO YOUR PRISON...

...WILL YOU EVER RETURN BY THE SAME ROAD TO FREEDOM?

SAVARKAR WENT IN. THE GATE WAS SHUT BEHIND HIM. HE FELT HE HAD ENTERED THE JAWS OF DEATH.

THE JAILOR WAS ONE MR. BARRIE.

ARE YOU THE ONE WHO TRIED TO ESCAPE AT MARSEILLES?

YES.

WHY DID YOU DO IT?

TO FREE MYSELF.

FOR YOUR OWN GOOD DO NOT TRY TO RUN AWAY. THE PRISON IS SURROUNDED ON ALL SIDES BY DENSE FORESTS. THE ABORIGINES WHO LIVE IN THE FORESTS ARE FIERCE.

IF THEY CATCH YOU THEY'LL KILL YOU AND EAT YOU.

I REALISE THAT PORT BLAIR IS NOT MARSEILLES.

TAKE HIM TO HIS CELL.

FOR THE FIRST FORTNIGHT SAVARKAR WAS CONFINED TO A SOLITARY CELL.

THE FIRST JOB HE WAS GIVEN WAS THE WORK OF CHOPPING THE BARK OF COCONUT TREES, WITH A CHISEL AND A HEAVY WOODEN MALLET.

LATER—

SAVARKAR, YOU HAVE BEEN GIVEN A PROMOTION. YOU WILL NOW WORK ON THE OIL MILL.

WORKING THE OIL CRUSHER WAS A STRENUOUS, TEDIOUS, AND FATIGUING TASK.

HIS BODY ACHED. HE FELT DIZZY.

WATER!

WATER!

A PRISONER IS GIVEN ONLY TWO CUPS OF WATER. YOU HAVE ALREADY CONSUMED THREE! AND YOU ASK FOR MORE!!!

GET ON WITH THE WORK!

WHEN IT WAS TIME FOR LUNCH SAVARKAR LEFT THE MILL WITH A SIGH.

HARDLY HAD HE EATEN TWO OR THREE MORSELS WHEN—

HAVEN'T YOU FINISHED YET? HURRY UP!

WITHOUT RESTING, SAVARKAR AND THE OTHERS WENT BACK TO THE MILL.

WHEN IT WAS EVENING—

THE OIL YOU HAVE EXTRACTED DOES NOT COMPLETE YOUR QUOTA.

YOU WILL CONTINUE TO WORK AFTER DINNER.

SO, LATE INTO THE NIGHT THE PRISONER SLOGGED, WHILE THE JAILOR SNORED.

SAVARKAR WAS ALLOWED TO RECEIVE AND WRITE ONE LETTER A YEAR FROM THE ANDAMANS. THIS IS AN EXTRACT FROM ONE OF HIS LETTERS TO HIS YOUNGER BROTHER, DR. N.D. SAVARKAR—

CELLULAR JAIL
9—3—1915
PORT BLAIR

BEST BELOVED BAL,

ONCE AGAIN, MY PEN HASTENS TO ACKNOWLEDGE THE RECEIPT OF YOUR LETTER RECEIVED SOME 7-8 MONTHS AGO. TO HAVE A LETTER FROM YOU IS LIKE SEEING YOU.

AS FAR AS OUR DAILY LIFE IS CONCERNED, WELL, IT GOES ON IN THE SAME EVEN WAY AS IT DID LAST YEAR. IN A PRISON WHAT HAPPENS ON THE FIRST DAY HAPPENS ALWAYS— IF NOTHING WORSE HAPPENS. IN FACT IT SEEMS TO BE THE ESSENCE OF PRISON DISCIPLINE TO AVOID ALL NOVELTY, ALL CHANGE. LIKE SPECIMENS AND CURIOS IN A MUSEUM HERE WE ARE EACH EXACTLY IN THE SAME PLACE AND SAME POSITION, BOTTLED AND LABELLED WITH THE SAME NUMBERS WITH MORE OR LESS DUST ABOUT US.

WHAT I WROTE TO YOU IN MY LAST LETTER MAY SERVE THE PURPOSE OF DESCRIPTION AS LONG AS I AM HERE. WE GET UP EARLY, WORK HARD, EAT PUNCTUALLY— AT THE SAME TIME, AT THE SAME PLACE AND THE SAME AMOUNT AND KIND OF FOOD PREPARED WITH THE SAME MATCHLESS PRISON-SKILL AND HYGIENE. ALTHOUGH IT IS TRUE THAT PRISONERS ARE NOT FREE TO DO OR SAY WHAT THEY WILL, YET, TO THE CREDIT OF THE JAIL AUTHORITIES, IT MUST BE ADMITTED THAT EVERY ONE IS ABSOLUTELY FREE TO DREAM WHAT HE LIKES. AND I ASSURE YOU I TAKE THE FULLEST ADVANTAGE OF THIS CONCESSION. ALMOST EVERY NIGHT, I TELL YOU, I BREAK JAIL AND GO ROMPING THROUGH DALE AND DOWN AND TOWER AND TOWN, TILL I FIND ONE OF YOU— SOMEONE WHO SOMEWHERE HAD BEEN HELD CLOSE TO MY BOSOM! EVERY NIGHT I DO IT BUT MY BENEFICENT JAILORS TAKE NO NOTICE OF IT. YOU HAVE ONLY TO WAKE UP IN THE JAIL, THAT IS ALL THEY SAY.

YOUR OWN BROTHER
TATYA

ONE DAY, WHILE HE WAS TURNING THE MILL —

END IT ALL! TO LIVE IS FUTILE! TO DIE IS HONOUR!

THE IDEA OF SUICIDE BEGAN TO HAUNT HIM. BUT REASON ULTIMATELY PREVAILED.

TO BEAR AND ENDURE TORTURE IS ALSO PART OF NATIONAL WORK. STAY ON AND FIGHT, FIGHT AT BAY IF YOU MUST.

HOWEVER, NOT ALL HAD THE STRENGTH OF SAVARKAR. INDU BHUSHAN ROY COMMITTED SUICIDE; ULLASKAR DUTT WENT MAD AND A KIND WORD WAS ENOUGH TO MOVE UPENDRANATH BANERJEE TO TEARS.

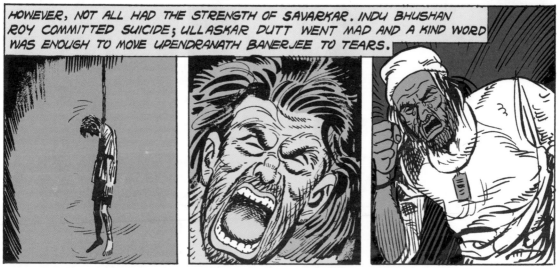

IT WAS LEFT TO SAVARKAR TO CHEER UP THE SILENT, SUFFERING POLITICAL PRISONERS.

DON'T DESPAIR, FRIENDS. DON'T GIVE UP. OUR SUFFERINGS WILL BE FRUITFUL IN THE END.

FUTURE GENERATIONS WILL MAKE A PILIGRIMAGE TO THIS PLACE SAYING- HERE DWELT FOR YEARS THE PATRIOTS OF OUR LAND, THE FLESH OF OUR FLESH, THE SPIRIT OF OUR SPIRIT THAT FELL IN THE CAUSE OF FREEDOM.

SAVARKAR WAS SUBJECTED TO VARIOUS KINDS OF TORTURE IN THE CELLULAR JAIL.

HE WAS PUT IN CHAINS...

....IN BACK HANDCUFFS...

....IN BARE FETTERS WHICH WOULD PREVENT HIM FROM BENDING...

....IN CROSS-BAR FETTERS WHICH COMPELLED HIM TO KEEP HIS FEET APART WHILE STANDING, SITTING, WALKING OR SLEEPING...

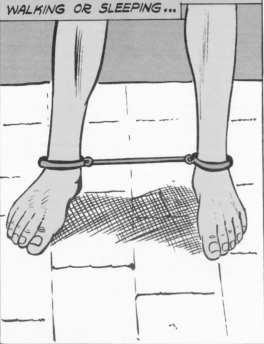

...AND HE WAS MADE TO STAND WITH HIS HANDS LOCKED UP TO A HOOK IN THE WALL MEASURING HIS HEIGHT.

YET HE BORE IT ALL WITH EQUANIMITY, WITH HIS MIND VERY ALERT, COMPOSING POEMS AND MEMORISING THE POEMS COMPOSED.

SAVARKAR CAME TO KNOW THAT HIS ELDER BROTHER GANESHRAO WAS SERVING TIME IN THE SAME PRISON.

SIR, COULD I MEET MY BROTHER?

WHO TOLD YOU YOUR BROTHER WAS HERE?

FINALLY, A KIND-HEARTED JAMADAR AGREED TO HELP.

NOW YOUR BROTHER'S BATCH IS ANSWERING THE ROLL CALL. YOURS WILL BE THE NEXT BATCH.

AS THE FIRST BATCH WENT BACK TO THE CELL MAKING WAY FOR THE SECOND BATCH TO ANSWER THE ROLL CALL —

TATYA! YOU? HERE?

GANESHRAO WAS SHOCKED TO KNOW THAT HIS BROTHER WAS SERVING HIS SENTENCE IN THE SAME PLACE.

DADA...!

HURRY UP! HURRY UP!

AS ABRUPTLY AS THEY HAD MET, THE BROTHERS HAD TO PART.

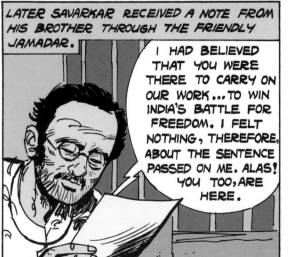

LATER SAVARKAR RECEIVED A NOTE FROM HIS BROTHER THROUGH THE FRIENDLY JAMADAR.

I HAD BELIEVED THAT YOU WERE THERE TO CARRY ON OUR WORK... TO WIN INDIA'S BATTLE FOR FREEDOM. I FELT NOTHING, THEREFORE, ABOUT THE SENTENCE PASSED ON ME. ALAS! YOU TOO, ARE HERE.

SAVARKAR REPLIED—

WE ARE DOOMED TO ROT AND DIE HERE... WE HAVE SERVED OUR COUNTRY BY OUR FAILURE. LET OTHERS SERVE HER BY THEIR SUCCESS...

TO THIS END SAVARKAR BEGAN EDUCATING HIS FELLOW POLITICAL PRISONERS.

BUT SAVARKAR, I HAVE NO USE FOR EDUCATION... I BELIEVE IN ACTION.

ASK ME TO THROW A BOMB, I WILL. ASK ME TO READ A BOOK, I'LL RUN AWAY.

OUTSIDE THE PRISON, YOU FOUGHT FOR FREEDOM.

INSIDE, YOU MUST PREPARE FOR THE RESPONSIBILITIES YOU WILL HAVE TO SHOULDER WHEN WE ATTAIN FREEDOM.

SAVARKAR HAD NO DOUBT WHAT-SOEVER THAT SOONER OR LATER THE COUNTRY WOULD BECOME FREE.

WHEN OUR COUNTRY BECOMES FREE WE WILL NEED ECONOMISTS, ADMINISTRATORS AND STATESMEN.

ALL RIGHT! ALL RIGHT! BUT WHERE ARE THE BOOKS?

AND WHO WILL GIVE US PAPER AND PEN?

WE'LL TRY TO GET THE BOOKS. FOR THE TIME BEING WE'LL USE THE PRISON WALLS.

PRISON WALLS?

YES. MY FRIENDS, TOMORROW WE HAVE TO CHANGE OUR CELLS. WHOEVER MOVES INTO CELL 7 PLEASE LOOK AT THE WALL.

THE FOLLOWING DAY A PRISONER WHO MOVED INTO CELL 7 LOOKED AT THE WALL.

MY GOD! IT IS FILLED WITH WRITING!

SAVARKAR HAD SCRATCHED OUT A COMPLETE LESSON ON THE PRINCIPLES OF DEMOCRACY.

A NEW ARRIVAL IN THE ANDAMANS, THROWN INTO A CELL, WAS LONELY, SAD AND DEJECTED. HE HAPPENED TO LOOK AT THE WALL.

FOR THY SAKE DEATH IS LIFE, WITHOUT THEE LIFE IS DEATH.

THAT WAS THE POEM SCRIBBLED BY SAVARKAR BEFORE HE WAS REMOVED TO ANOTHER CELL. IT WAS A POEM ADDRESSED TO MOTHER INDIA.

YES! O MOTHER, WHO WILL DARE INSULT THEE IN THE WORLD? WE WILL GIVE THEE A BATH OF HIS BLOOD.

SAVARKAR AND HIS FRIENDS BEGAN TO COMMUNICATE THROUGH "TELEGRAPH!" THEIR TELEGRAPH CONSISTED OF SOUNDS MADE BY THE TINGLING NOISE OF THE FETTERS THAT BOUND THEM.

SAVARKAR AND HIS FRIENDS CONTINUED TO TOIL. ONE DAY, NANI GOPAL, A BENGALI REVOLUTIONARY, STRUCK WORK.

NO. I WON'T RUN THE MILL.

WHAT!

NANI GOPAL WANTED TO BE RECOGNISED AS A POLITICAL PRISONER. HE REFUSED TO ANSWER QUESTIONS. WHEN PUNISHED, HE REFUSED TO PUT ON CLOTHES.

MEANWHILE, SOME PRISONERS HAD MANAGED TO SMUGGLE OUT LETTERS COMPLAINING ABOUT THE ILL TREATMENT METED OUT TO THEM. THESE LETTERS REACHED THE OUTSIDE WORLD AND NEWSPAPERS PUBLISHED THEM. THE GOVERNMENT WAS COMPELLED TO TAKE NOTICE.

SAVARKAR, SIR REGINALD CRADDOCK IS COMING TO VISIT THE JAIL.

IT'S HIGH TIME HE DID.

CRADDOCK WENT ROUND THE JAIL AND LATER HAD A TALK WITH SAVARKAR.

WE ARE MUCH KINDER THAN YOU REALISE MR. SAVARKAR. HAD YOU REVOLTED AGAINST YOUR RAJAS, THEY WOULD HAVE HAD YOU TRAMPLED BY ELEPHANTS.

FOR THAT MATTER, IN THE DAYS YOU SPEAK OF, A MAN IN ENGLAND WOULD HAVE BEEN BEHEADED FOR COMMITTING A THEFT.

BESIDES, REBELS WERE NO DOUBT TRAMPLED UNDER AN ELEPHANT. BUT IF THE REBELS EMERGED VICTORIOUS THE KING WOULD LOSE HIS HEAD — AS IT HAPPENED TO YOUR OWN KING, CHARLES I.

CRADDOCK WENT AWAY. NANI GOPAL CONTINUED WITH HIS HUNGER STRIKE.

NANI GOPAL IS ON THE VERGE OF DYING. THERE IS ONLY ONE WAY TO MAKE HIM GIVE UP.

SAVARKAR HIMSELF WENT ON A HUNGER STRIKE.

SAVARKAR, I FEEL GUILTY THAT YOU HAVE GIVEN UP FOOD ON ACCOUNT OF ME.

WELL, NANI, IF YOU BREAK YOUR FAST, I TOO WILL EAT.

IF YOU MUST DIE, DIE FIGHTING LIKE A HERO.

TAKE AS MUCH FOOD FROM THEM AS YOU CAN, GROW FAT AND DON'T WORK.

NANI GOPAL GAVE UP HIS HUNGER STRIKE. AND THE PRISONERS STRUCK WORK. THEY REFUSED TO RUN THE HATED OIL MILL.

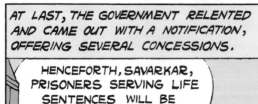

AT LAST, THE GOVERNMENT RELENTED AND CAME OUT WITH A NOTIFICATION, OFFERING SEVERAL CONCESSIONS.

HENCEFORTH, SAVARKAR, PRISONERS SERVING LIFE SENTENCES WILL BE DETAINED IN THE ANDAMANS FOR ONLY 14 YEARS.

SAVARKAR SMILED.

IN MY CASE, TWENTY-EIGHT YEARS! I AM SERVING A DOUBLE SENTENCE!

AFTER WORLD WAR I ENDED, A ROYAL PROCLAMATION WAS ISSUED DECLARING CLEMENCY TO POLITICAL PRISONERS. JAILS WERE THROWN OPEN AND POLITICAL PRISONERS WALKED OUT.

BUT SAVARKAR CONTINUED TO ROT IN THE ANDAMANS. HE WAS CONSIDERED TOO DANGEROUS TO BE FREED.

THREE YEARS LATER, IN 1921, SAVARKAR AND HIS BROTHER WERE REMOVED FROM THE ANDAMANS...

...AND BROUGHT BY SHIP...

...TO THE MAINLAND.

VANDE MATARAM!

THE GOVERNMENT CONSIDERED SAVARKAR 'A DANGER TO THE PEACE OF INDIA'. HE WAS INTERNED AND WAS SET FREE UNCONDITIONALLY ONLY IN 1937. SAVARKAR TOOK AN ACTIVE PART IN THE STRUGGLE FOR FREEDOM. HE HAD THE SATISFACTION OF WITNESSING THE TRICOLOUR UNFURLED ON AUGUST 15, 1947.

Suppandi and his friends are all packed!

We introduce our Tinkle Toon Collections and
Amar Chitra Katha comics to make your travel more fun.

www.amarchitrakatha.com

Make sure you're packed. Log on to our website now to
buy any comic or picture book with your special 20%
discount code: 'ACK 20', and have your favourite travel
companions delivered straight to your doorstep.

TINKLE |

SUBHAS CHANDRA BOSE

BORN TO LEAD

www.amarchitrakatha.com

The route to your roots

SUBHAS CHANDRA BOSE

'Jai Hind!' Subhas Chandra Bose's stirring war cry brought hope to Indians everywhere. Indian soldiers in Japanese prisoners-of-war camps as well as freedom-loving youth in the country were infected by his call to arms. Though born to wealth and comfort, this brilliant scholar was also a born leader. His ideas and efforts went a long way in gaining India her freedom from British rule.

<table>
<tr><td>**Script**
Yagya Sharma &
Haridas Shetty</td><td>**Illustrations**
H. S. Chavan &
Sailo Chakravarty</td><td>**Editor**
Anant Pai</td></tr>
</table>

Cover illustration by: Pratap Mulick

SUBHAS CHANDRA BOSE

SUBHAS CHANDRA BOSE
WAS BORN IN CUTTACK,
ORISSA, ON JANUARY
23, 1897. HIS MOTHER
WAS PRABHAVATI AND
HIS FATHER, THE FAMOUS
LAWYER, JANAKI NATH
BOSE.

WHEN SUBHAS WAS FIVE, HE WAS ADMITTED TO THE PROTESTANT EUROPEAN SCHOOL, AT CUTTACK.

HE SOON BECAME A FAVOURITE OF THE TEACHERS.

THAT BOY WITH THE BOOK IS SUBHAS, A BRILLIANT BOY!

HIS ELDER BROTHERS TOO WENT TO THE SAME SCHOOL. ONE DAY—

HAVE YOU HEARD? BENGALI HAS BEEN MADE COMPULSORY FOR BENGALEES AT THE MATRIC LEVEL.

BUT BENGALI IS NOT TAUGHT AT OUR SCHOOL.

SUBHAS WHO WAS NOW TWELVE YEARS OLD, WAS TRANSFERRED TO RAVENSHAW COLLEGIATE SCHOOL.

SO YOU HAVE NEVER LEARNT BENGALI.

NO. BUT I SOON WILL, SIR.

ON THE VERY FIRST DAY AT THE NEW SCHOOL—

FROM TOMORROW I SHALL DRESS LIKE THEM.

THE NEXT DAY AS SUBHAS WAS LEAVING FOR SCHOOL, HIS FATHER SAW HIM

WHY? WHAT IS THE MATTER? WHY ARE YOU GOING TO SCHOOL DRESSED LIKE THIS?

THIS IS HOW THEY ALL DRESS AT THE NEW SCHOOL, FATHER.

BENI MADHAV DAS, THE HEAD MASTER, WAS A TRUE NATIONALIST.

NEVER FORGET, WE ARE INDIANS AND INDIA IS A GREAT COUNTRY. WHILE YOU LEARN YOUR LESSONS, LEARN TO LOVE YOUR COUNTRY TOO.

A FEW MONTHS LATER, ON THE EVE OF THE FIRST ANNIVERSARY OF THE MARTYRDOM OF KSHUDIRAM BOSE WHO WAS HANGED ON AUGUST 11, 1910

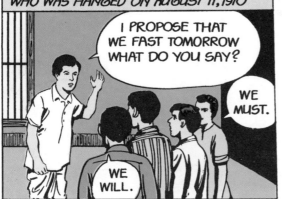

I PROPOSE THAT WE FAST TOMORROW WHAT DO YOU SAY?

WE MUST.

WE WILL.

BENI MADHAV DAS DID NOT SAY A WORD TO THE BOYS, BUT HE WAS PROUD OF THEM. HE TOO FASTED.

THE BRITISH GOVERNMENT DID NOT LIKE THAT AND BENI MADHAV DAS WAS TRANSFERRED TO BENGAL.

YOU ARE DESTINED TO BE GREAT, SUBHAS MAY GOD BLESS YOU.

SUBHAS HUNG A PHOTOGRAPH OF BENI MADHAV DAS IN THE SCHOOL HALL.

WE MUST NEVER FORGET WHAT HE TAUGHT US. WE MUST LIVE UP TO ALL THAT HE STANDS FOR.

ACCORDINGLY, WHEN A SMALL-POX EPIDEMIC HIT A VILLAGE, SUBHAS FORMED A VOLUNTEER CORPS WITH HIS FRIENDS TO NURSE THE POOR AND NEGLECTED PATIENTS.

THEY ARE OUR BROTHERS THEY NEED HELP. LET US HELP THEM.

AT THE AGE OF FIFTEEN, SUBHAS BEGAN READING THE WORKS OF SWAMI VIVEKANANDA.

HOW NOBLE AND INSPIRING.

AT LAST I HAVE FOUND THE ANSWERS TO MANY OF MY QUESTIONS.

AT ABOUT THE SAME TIME SUBHAS STARTED PRACTISING YOGA TOO.

BUT HE WAS STILL RESTLESS.

I NEED A GURU TO GUIDE ME TO MY DESTINY.

MEANWHILE, SUBHAS PASSED HIS MATRICULATION EXAMINATION.

FATHER, I HAVE STOOD SECOND IN THE UNIVERSITY.

MAY GOD BLESS YOU, MY BOY.

SUBHAS WENT TO CALCUTTA WHERE HE SECURED ADMISSION TO THE PRESIDENCY COLLEGE. ON HIS WAY HOME—

ACADEMIC KNOWLEDGE IS PASSIVE...

...WHEREAS THE SPIRITUAL WELFARE AND THE PROSPERITY OF MY COUNTRY NEED DYNAMISM.

YOUNG SUBHAS'S YEARNING FOR A GURU BECAME VERY STRONG. HE SPOKE ABOUT IT TO A LIKE-MINDED FRIEND.

WE MUST GO IN SEARCH OF A GURU.

YES! ONE WHO CAN SHOW US THE RIGHT PATH.

SO, ACCOMPANIED BY THE FRIEND, SUBHAS VISITED MANY PILGRIM CENTRES, HOPING TO FIND A TRUE GURU.

BUT IT PROVED TO BE A FUTILE SEARCH.

THESE SO-CALLED SAINTS ARE INTERESTED MORE IN WORLDLY MATTERS THAN IN SPIRITUALISM.

DISILLUSIONED, SUBHAS RETURNED HOME TO CALCUTTA.

SUBHAS, YOU CAN STILL PURSUE YOUR IDEAL. YOU MAY HAVE TO DO IT WITHOUT A SPIRITUAL GUIDE.

I HAVE REALISED THAT, FATHER.

SUBHAS WENT TO COLLEGE. THE RUDE BEHAVIOUR OF THE BRITISH TEACHERS THERE WAS HUMILIATING TO THE INDIAN STUDENTS.

YOU NATIVES HAVE NOTHING IN YOUR BRAINS BUT SAWDUST.

PROFESSOR OTEN'S REMARK AT A COLLEGE MEETING WAS THE LAST STRAW.

YOU ARE BARBARIANS! IT IS WE ENGLISH WHO HAVE CIVILIZED YOU.

WE HAVE TOLERATED ENOUGH WE MUST PROTEST.

SUBHAS LED A BATCH OF STUDENTS TO THE PRINCIPAL'S ROOM. THE PRINCIPAL, MR JAMES, WAS ALSO AN ENGLISHMAN.

SIR, PROFESSOR OTEN'S BEHAVIOUR IS RUDE AND UNWARRANTED.

HOW DARE YOU CRITICIZE YOUR TEACHER GO AND BEG HIS FORGIVENESS.

THE STUDENTS WERE APPALLED.

HE INSULTED US AND WE HAVE TO ASK HIS FORGIVENESS! THIS IS MOST UNJUST.

WE MUST DO SOMETHING...

...BUT DO IT WITH CAUTION.

SUBHAS TOOK THE LEAD AND CALLED FOR A STRIKE. OVER A THOUSAND STUDENTS PARTICIPATED. NO CLASSES COULD BE HELD. THIS WAS THE FIRST STRIKE IN MODERN INDIA.

WE DEMAND BETTER TREATMENT BOYCOTT THE CLASSES.

BOYCOTT CLASSES

IT WENT ON FOR THREE DAYS. THE INDIAN TEACHERS ALSO SUPPORTED IT. AT LAST—

HURRAH! PROFESSOR OTEN HAS APOLOGISED.

LET'S CALL OFF THE STRIKE.

BUT PROFESSOR OTEN NEVER FORGAVE THE BOYS. ONE DAY—

CAN'T YOU WALK WITHOUT FLAPPING YOUR SLIPPERS?

SUBHAS RETURNED TO CUTTACK.

IT IS HEARTENING TO KNOW THAT MY PARENTS THINK I DID THE RIGHT THING.

DURGA PUJA WAS APPROACHING. SUBHAS ORGANISED A PUBLIC PUJA CEREMONY WITH HIS FRIENDS.

THEY FED THE POOR AND...

...FORMED A "NURSING BROTHERHOOD" TO RENDER SERVICE TO NEGLECTED PATIENTS.

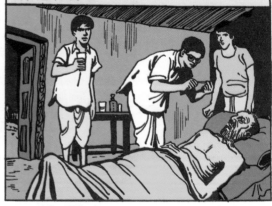

SUBHAS SOON BECAME A POPULAR FIGURE.

WHY DON'T YOU GO BACK TO COLLEGE?

SIR ASUTOSH MUKHERJI, VICE-CHANCELLOR OF CALCUTTA UNIVERSITY, WAS HELPFUL.

THE UNIVERSITY WILL HAVE NO OBJECTION IF THE PRINCIPAL OF ANY COLLEGE ADMITS HIM.

AFTER PERSISTENT EFFORTS, HE GAINED ADMISSION IN THE SCOTTISH CHURCH COLLEGE.

I'M GLAD, I DECIDED TO JOIN THE UNIVERSITY TRAINING CORPS. THIS MILITARY TRAINING IT OFFERS WILL BE USEFUL... WHEN WE FIGHT THE BRITISH.

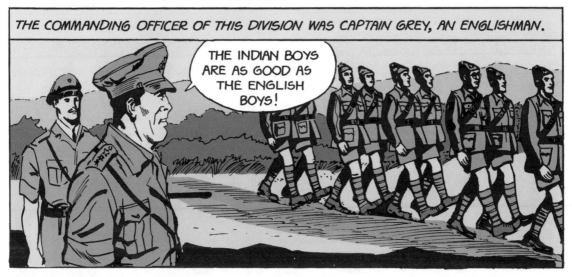

THE COMMANDING OFFICER OF THIS DIVISION WAS CAPTAIN GREY, AN ENGLISHMAN.

THE INDIAN BOYS ARE AS GOOD AS THE ENGLISH BOYS!

AT THAT TIME PROFESSOR OTEN HAPPENED TO BE THE DIRECTOR OF PUBLIC INSTRUCTION IN BENGAL. HE CAME TO VISIT THE TRAINING CAMP.
ONE DAY—

IT'S HIM. WILL HE TAKE REVENGE ON ME?

THAT BOY, CAPTAIN, IS HE ANY GOOD?

BOSE, SIR? WELL HE'S ONE OF THE BEST.

AFTER THE PARADE —

BOSE, YOUR CAPTAIN SPEAKS HIGHLY OF YOU.

I OFFER YOU A NON-COMMISSIONED OFFICER'S POST IN THE CORPS.

THANK YOU, SIR.

IT'S A GREAT HONOUR. I AM GRATEFUL TO YOU, SIR.

SUBHAS GRADUATED FROM CALCUTTA UNIVERSITY AT THE AGE OF 22 AND WENT TO ENGLAND TO APPEAR FOR THE INDIAN CIVIL SERVICE EXAMINATION.

YOU ARE DOING WELL. KEEP IT UP, MY BOY.

THANK YOU, SIR.

HE PASSED THE EXAMINATION WITH MERIT.

CONGRATULATIONS. YOU HAVE STOOD FOURTH. YOU HAVE A BRIGHT FUTURE AHEAD OF YOU.

THANK YOU...

...BUT I PLAN TO RESIGN FROM THE SERVICE.

WHY?

I APPEARED FOR MY I.C.S. EXAMINATION TO EDUCATE MYSELF— NOT TO BECOME A PART OF THE BUREAUCRATIC MACHINE OF THE BRITISH EMPIRE.

SOON AFTERWARDS SUBHAS RETURNED TO INDIA.

YOUR RESIGNATION HAS CREATED A SENSATION. WHAT DO YOU PROPOSE TO DO NOW?

WORK TO FREE MY COUNTRY.

IMMEDIATELY AFTER LANDING AT BOMBAY, HE MET MAHATMA GANDHI AND TALKED ABOUT THE FREEDOM STRUGGLE. BUT—

SUBHAS, MY ROAD TO FREEDOM IS A NON-VIOLENT ONE.

NON-VIOLENCE IS GOOD IN PRINCIPLE, BUT...

I KNOW YOUR IDEAS. I SUGGEST YOU SEE DESHABANDHU CHITTARANJAN DAS AND WORK WITH HIM.

DESHABANDHU CHITTARANJAN DAS WAS THE UNCROWNED KING OF BENGAL. SUBHAS CAME TO CALCUTTA AND MET HIM.

WELCOME, SUBHAS.

I HAVE FOUND MY LEADER.

SOON SUBHAS BECAME AN ACTIVE WORKER AND THE RIGHT HAND MAN OF DESHABANDHU.

FOR A LIVING HE TOOK ON THE PRINCIPALSHIP OF THE NATIONAL COLLEGE AT CALCUTTA.

ON DECEMBER 10, 1921, HE WAS ARRESTED FOR THE FIRST TIME FOR ANTI-GOVERNMENT ACTIVITIES.

I SENTENCE YOU TO SIX MONTHS' SIMPLE IMPRISON- MENT.

A MERE SIX MONTHS! I'M NO COMMON THIEF.

DESHASANDHU HAD DIFFERENCES OF OPINION WITH OTHER LEADERS OF THE CONGRESS. HE DECIDED TO FORM A NEW PARTY.

OUR "SWARAJ PARTY" WILL WORK WITHIN THE CONGRESS PARTY.

LATER, WHEN IN THE MONTH OF APRIL 1924, THE CALCUTTA CORPORATION ELECTIONS WERE HELD, THE SWARAJ PARTY BAGGED ALMOST ALL THE SEATS.

SWARAJ PARTY ZINDABAD.

LONG LIVE SWARAJ PARTY

DESHABANDHU WAS ELECTED THE MAYOR AND SUBHAS WAS APPOINTED THE CHIEF EXECUTIVE OFFICER OF THE CALCUTTA CORPORATION.

THE SWARAJ PARTY HAS PERFORMED A MIRACLE.

THINGS ARE CHANGING FAST.

THE SWARAJISTS INTRODUCED MANY CHANGES IN THE ADMINISTRATION. KHADI WAS MADE THE OFFICIAL DRESS OF THE CORPORATION WORKERS.

SUBHAS, AS THE CHIEF EXECUTIVE OFFICER, PERSONALLY INSPECTED THE WORK OF THE MUNICIPAL STAFF ON THE STREETS.

SEE, THE C.E.O. HIMSELF IS HERE AT SUCH AN EARLY HOUR.

UNDER THE GUIDANCE OF CHITTARANJAN DAS, SUBHAS FORMED A VOLUNTEER CORPS TO SELL KHADI AND DO OTHER SOCIAL AND POLITICAL WORK. BUT—

CHITTARANJAN BABU! THE VOLUNTEER CORPS HAS BEEN DECLARED ILLEGAL. THERE MUST BE NO DEMONSTRATIONS, PROCESSIONS OR MEETINGS.

SUBHAS STARTED SENDING FIVE VOLUNTEERS EVERY DAY FOR DEMONSTRATIONS.

WEAR KHADI!

USE NATIONAL GOODS!

BOYCOTT FOREIGN GOODS!

THE ATMOSPHERE IN CALCUTTA WAS VERY TENSE. ONE DAY—

SENSATIONAL! HOT NEWS! ONE EUROPEAN MURDERED. GOPINATH SAHA ARRESTED.

THE GOVERNMENT GOT A CHANCE TO ARREST SUBHAS AGAIN ON A FALSE PRETEXT.

MR. BOSE, YOU ARE ARRESTED FOR MASTERMINDING THE MURDER OF THE EUROPEAN.

I PROTEST! I HAD NOTHING TO DO WITH IT.

DEMONSTRATIONS FOLLOWED THE ARREST OF SUBHAS.

SHAME! SHAME! FREE SUBHAS BOSE IMMEDIATELY. SUBHAS BOSE ZINDABAD!

FRIGHTENED BY THE MOOD OF THE PUBLIC, THE BRITISH GOVERNMENT SENT SUBHAS TO MANDALAY JAIL IN BURMA.

I AM BEING PUNISHED WITHOUT EVEN A TRIAL FOR A CRIME I DID NOT COMMIT. THIS IS INJUSTICE.

THE JAIL WAS HORRIBLE THERE WAS NO SHELTER FROM THE RAIN OR THE HOT SUN.

IS THIS A PRISON FOR MEN OR A CAGE FOR BEASTS?

UNDER THE INHUMAN, UNHEALTHY CONDITIONS, SUBHAS FELL ILL.

COUGH... COUGH...

SUBHAS CONTRACTED TUBERCULOSIS. IT RUINED HIS HEALTH.

HIS CONDITION IS SERIOUS.

VERY BAD INDEED.

THE NEWS SPREAD IN CALCUTTA LIKE WILDFIRE.

RELEASE HIM AT ONCE. LONG LIVE SUBHAS BOSE.

THE GOVERNMENT HAS AGREED TO RELEASE YOU ON CONDITION THAT YOU WILL LEAVE IMMEDIATELY FOR EUROPE.

I REFUSE CONDITIONAL FREEDOM. I WOULD RATHER DIE HERE.

GRADUALLY HIS CONDITION BECAME ALARMING AND THE GOVERNMENT RELEASED HIM UNCONDITIONALLY.

MR. BOSE, YOU ARE RELEASED. THE BRITISH GOVERNMENT IS KIND.

SO KIND THAT IT SENDS INNOCENT MEN TO JAIL.

AFTER HIS RELEASE HE SPENT SOME TIME AT DALHOUSIE IN THE HILLS, RECOUPING HIS HEALTH.

DESHABANDHU IS NO MORE. BUT WE OWE IT TO HIM TO FREE OUR COUNTRY.

IN 1928, THE INDIAN NATIONAL CONGRESS HELD ITS SESSION IN CALCUTTA. SUBHAS ORGANISED A VOLUNTEER CORPS ON THE OCCASION AND BECAME ITS GENERAL OFFICER COMMANDING.

YOU HAVE A HARD TASK, INDEED.

THE GOVERNMENT WAS SUSPICIOUS OF SUBHAS AND HIS VOLUNTEERS.

MR. BOSE, YOU ARE ARRESTED. YOU WORK AGAINST HIS MAJESTY'S GOVERNMENT.

I KNOW I AM CAUSING CONCERN TO HIS MAJESTY.

WHILE IN JAIL, HE WAS ELECTED THE MAYOR OF CALCUTTA CORPORATION IN 1931.

RELEASE HIM IMMEDIATELY. HE IS OUR MAYOR.

SUBHAS WAS RELEASED AND TOOK UP HIS DUTIES AS THE MAYOR OF CALCUTTA.

HE PLANNED PUBLIC MEETINGS AND PROCESSIONS FOR "INDEPENDENCE DAY" – JANUARY 26. BUT–

PROCESSIONS AND MEETINGS ARE BANNED. THEY ARE ILLEGAL.

SUBHAS LED A PROCESSION FROM THE CORPORATION BUILDING. BUT THE POLICE AND THEIR LATHIS CAUGHT UP WITH IT.

SUBHAS BOSE ZINDABAD!

HE WAS IN JAIL AGAIN, THIS TIME AT INSIN NEAR RANGOON. ONCE AGAIN HE FELL ILL.

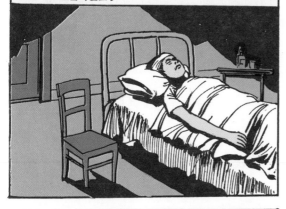

HIS CONDITION DETERIORATED.

SUBHAS, THEY ARE AGITATING FOR YOUR RELEASE ALL OVER INDIA.

HE WAS RELEASED. HE PROCEEDED TO EUROPE FOR TREATMENT. AT VIENNA...

...HIS HEALTH GRADUALLY IMPROVED AND HE TOURED MANY COUNTRIES OF EUROPE TO PROMOTE THE CAUSE OF INDIAN FREEDOM.

WHEN HE HEARD THAT HIS FATHER WAS ON HIS DEATH-BED IN CALCUTTA HE ARRIVED IN BOMBAY WITHOUT THE GOVERNMENT'S PERMISSION.

MR. BOSE, YOU ARE ARRESTED FOR VIOLATING THE GOVERNMENT ORDER.

I WANT TO BE NEAR MY DYING FATHER.

HIS FATHER DIED BEFORE SUBHAS COULD REACH CALCUTTA. HE WENT BACK TO EUROPE.

WHEN HE WAS ELECTED CONGRESS PRESIDENT AT THE HARIPURA SESSION IN 1938 HE WAS ALLOWED TO RETURN TO INDIA.

WAR IN EUROPE IS IMMINENT. THIS IS OUR CHANCE TO STRIKE AT THE BRITISH.

THE OTHER LEADERS, INCLUDING GANDHIJI, DID NOT AGREE. THEY OPPOSED HIS RE-ELECTION FOR THE NEXT SESSION AT TRIPURA IN 1939. BUT SUBHAS WON.

THE COUNTRY IS READY TO FIGHT.

BUT HIS VICTORY WAS NOT TO LAST LONG.

MY DIFFERENCES WITH THE MAHATMA WILL SPLIT THE PARTY. I MUST RESIGN.

WITHIN THREE DAYS OF HIS RESIGNATION HE FORMED THE **FORWARD BLOC** WITHIN THE CONGRESS PARTY.

WE DEMAND INDIAN INDEPENDENCE, HERE AND NOW.

ON THE THIRD OF JULY, WE SHALL DESTROY THE HOLWELL MONUMENT, WHICH IS A SYMBOL OF OUR SLAVERY.

HE WAS ARRESTED AND SENT TO JAIL.

ONLY AN ARMED STRUGGLE CAN SAVE INDIA. I NEED TO GO AND SEEK FOREIGN HELP FOR IT.

IN JAIL HE PLANNED HIS ESCAPE. HE STARTED FASTING.

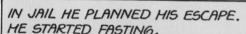

YOU MUST RELEASE ME OR I FAST UNTO DEATH.

AFRAID OF PUBLIC ANGER, THE GOVERNMENT RELEASED HIM BUT HIS HOUSE WAS HEAVILY GUARDED.

I HAVE TO GET OUT OF INDIA BY SOME MEANS.

ON THE MIDNIGHT OF JANUARY 7, 1941, A BEARDED MUSLIM CAME OUT IN A CHAUFFEURED BLACK CAR.

HE WAS SEEN NEXT IN A TRAIN IN A FIRST CLASS COMPARTMENT.

I AM MOULVI JIAUDDIN, AN INSURANCE AGENT.

IT WAS NONE OTHER THAN SUBHAS.

AT PESHAWAR, HE BECAME A DEAF AND DUMB PATHAN AND ACCOMPANIED ANOTHER PATHAN WHO WAS ALSO AN INDIAN IN DISGUISE.

I AM NOW RAHAMAT KHAN, SUBHAS BABU.

SUBHAS REACHED KABUL IN A LOADED LORRY.

FINALLY HE REACHED BERLIN VIA MOSCOW AND STARTED HECTIC ACTIVITIES TO LIBERATE INDIA.

THIS IS SUBHAS CHANDRA BOSE SPEAKING.

HE ORGANIZED THE INDIAN NATIONAL ARMY WITH INDIAN PRISONERS OF WAR AND FORMED THE INDIAN INDEPENDENCE LEAGUE.

I WILL RAISE A WELL-TRAINED ARMY, AND FIGHT THE BRITISH.

HE ALSO MET HITLER AND SOUGHT HIS HELP.

BUT GERMANY WAS TOO FAR OFF TO WAGE WAR AGAINST THE BRITISH IN INDIA.

I MUST GET THE JAPANESE ON TO THIS.

HE TRAVELLED BY A GERMAN SUBMARINE TO SOUTH EAST ASIA ON JANUARY 26, 1943.

HE THEN MOVED TO A JAPANESE SUBMARINE.

HE ARRIVED ON JUNE 13 IN TOKYO. FROM TOKYO HE CAME TO SINGAPORE, WHERE HE WAS RECEIVED BY RASH BEHARI BOSE AND OTHER REVOLUTIONARIES.

HERE SUBHAS RAISED AN ARMY WITH INDIAN PRISONERS OF WAR CAPTURED BY THE JAPANESE.

YOU WERE FIGHTING FOR AN ALIEN POWER. NOW, YOU SHALL FIGHT FOR YOUR OWN COUNTRY.

HE ALSO FORMED THE RANI OF JHANSI REGIMENT WITH INDIAN GIRLS, TO NURSE THE SOLDIERS.

HE ANNOUNCED THE FORMATION OF THE AZAD HIND GOVERNMENT ON OCTOBER 21, 1943.

IN INDIA WE HAVE MANY RELIGIONS AND DIFFERENT WAYS OF SALUTATION. BUT WITH US IT SHALL BE **JAI HIND**!

JAI HIND!

YOUR GOAL IS DELHI. ONWARD TO DELHI.

CHALO DELHI.

NETAJI ZINDABAD! NETAJI ZINDABAD!

GIVE ME BLOOD, I PROMISE YOU FREEDOM.

NETAJI ZINDABAD!

AT THE CALL OF SUBHAS, THE INDIAN RESIDENTS DONATED GENEROUSLY TO THE CAUSE.

HERE ARE MY ORNAMENTS.

I DONATE MY ENTIRE PROPERTY AND WISH TO JOIN THE **I.N.A.**.

HERE ARE MY SAVINGS.

LET US MARCH TO THE BATTLEFIELD. WE MAY DIE BUT OUR COUNTRY SHALL BE FREE.

JAI HIND.

NETAJI ZINDABAD!

ON MARCH 14, THE IMPHAL KOHIMA ROAD IN ASSAM WAS CUT OFF BY THE ADVANCING FORCES. IMPHAL WAS COMPLETELY SURROUNDED BY THE I.N.A. AND THE JAPANESE.

THE I.N.A. ENTERED KOHIMA ON MARCH 18, 1944.

JAI HIND!

AZAD HIND ZINDABAD.

NETAJI ZINDABAD!

BUT THE BRITISH RESISTANCE IN IMPHAL WAS STRONG AND UNYIELDING.

THE JAPANESE WERE RETREATING EVERYWHERE. THE I.N.A. DEPENDED ON JAPAN FOR ARMS AND FOOD. ITS SUPPLIES WERE CUT.

THE MESSAGE FROM THE JAPANESE SAYS "YOU CAN'T GET AIR SUPPORT. IT IS VITALLY NEEDED IN THE PACIFIC."

THEN THE HEAVY MONSOON BURST ON THEM. THE BRITISH THRUST FORWARD. THE INDIAN NATIONAL ARMY HAD TO RETREAT.

ON APRIL 24, SUBHAS BROADCAST TO HIS FRIENDS, SOLDIERS AND COUNTRYMEN.

COMRADES! AT THIS CRITICAL HOUR I HAVE ONLY ONE WORD FOR YOU AND THAT IS IF YOU HAVE TO GO DOWN TEMPORARILY, THEN GO DOWN FIGHTING WITH THE NATIONAL TRICOLOUR HELD ALOFT. GO DOWN AS HEROES, GO DOWN UPHOLDING THE HIGHEST CODE OF HONOUR AND DISCIPLINE. I HAVE ALWAYS SAID THAT THE DARKEST HOUR PRECEDES THE DAWN. WE ARE NOW PASSING THROUGH THE DARKEST HOUR; THEREFORE, THE DAWN IS NOT FAR OFF. INDIA SHALL BE FREE.

THE JAPANESE SURRENDERED TO THE BRITISH-AMERICAN FORCES. THE I.N.A. ALSO SURRENDERED ON AUGUST 16, 1945.

NETAJI'S LIFE WAS IN DANGER. THE BRITISH-AMERICAN FORCES WERE SEARCHING FOR HIM.

NETAJI, PLEASE LEAVE FOR A SAFE PLACE. IT'S RISKY HERE FOR YOU.

WAR IS A RISKY BUSINESS. DIDN'T YOU KNOW?

BUT WE NEED YOU SAFE—TO LEAD US AGAIN.

BUT NETAJI WOULD NOT LEAVE OR GIVE UP.

I WANT TO START AGAIN FROM SOME OTHER PLACE.

YES, NETAJI, THE TIME IS SHORT. WE CANNOT ALLOW YOU TO BE CAUGHT BY THE BRITISH.

ON AUGUST 17, NETAJI BOARDED A JAPANESE PLANE FOR SOME UNKNOWN DESTINATION WITH COL. HABIBUR RAHMAN.

JAI HIND!

NETAJI ZINDABAD! JAI HIND!

WHAT BECAME OF NETAJI ON THAT FATE-FUL TRIP IS A MYSTERY. IS HE DEAD? DOES HE LIVE? THERE IS NO ANSWER TO THESE QUESTIONS.

BHAGAT SINGH

THE CHEERFUL YOUNG MARTYR

www.amarchitrakatha.com

The route to your roots

BHAGAT SINGH

Bhagat Singh sang gustily as he walked to the gallows. Backed by a courageous family, this twenty-three-year-old firebrand was wedded to death. A free India was his heaven, and the martyrs of the freedom struggle were his gods. Using disguise and guile, persuasion and force, his life was a roller-coaster ride through an unjust system. But eventually, he awakened India and the world to the idea of liberty, and brought the mighty British Raj to its knees.

| **Script** | **Illustrations** | **Editor** |
| Rajinder Singh and Subba Rao | Dilip Kadam | Anant Pai |

Cover illustration by: Pratap Mulick

BHAGAT SINGH

SEPTEMBER 27, 1907: IN THE VILLAGE OF BANGA, NEAR LAHORE, THE BIRTH OF A BABY BROUGHT JOY TO THE OTHERWISE GLOOMY HOUSEHOLD OF SARDAR KISHAN SINGH.

VIDYAVATI LOOKED FONDLY AT HER BABY.

I WISH YOUR FATHER AND UNCLES WERE HERE TODAY.

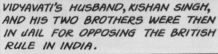

VIDYAVATI'S HUSBAND, KISHAN SINGH, AND HIS TWO BROTHERS WERE THEN IN JAIL FOR OPPOSING THE BRITISH RULE IN INDIA.

SOON AFTER—

KISHAN!

MOTHER!

KISHAN SINGH AND HIS YOUNGEST BROTHER, SWARAN SINGH, COULD COME HOME BECAUSE THEY WERE RELEASED ON BAIL.

IF ONLY AJIT, TOO, WERE HERE WITH US!

AJIT SINGH, THE SECOND BROTHER WAS SERVING A SENTENCE IN THE MANDALAY JAIL IN BURMA.

JUST THEN —

A TELEGRAM, SIR.

IT'S FROM MANDALAY! AJIT HAS BEEN RELEASED!

MY GRANDSON, YOU ARE THE BHAGANWALA, THE LUCKY ONE.

KISHAN, WHEN IS AJIT COMING HOME?

WELL... NOT IMMEDIATELY, I AM AFRAID. HE HAS LEFT FOR GERMANY.

MONTHS WENT BY.

WHY DOESN'T MY SON COME HOME?

MOTHER, PLEASE TRY TO UNDERSTAND. THE MOMENT AJIT RETURNS, HE'LL BE JAILED AGAIN ON SOME PRETEXT OR OTHER.

I UNDERSTAND. BUT MY POOR DAUGHTER-IN-LAW. WHO WILL WIPE HER TEARS?

AS TIME WENT BY, AJIT SINGH'S EXILE HAD ITS IMPACT ON LITTLE BHAGAT SINGH.

MOTHER, WHY DOES AUNTIE WEEP ALL THE TIME?

SHE MISSES YOUR UNCLE.

WHY DOESN'T HE COME HOME, THEN?

HE CAN'T, MY SON. OUR COUNTRY IS RULED BY THE BRITISH. YOUR UNCLE WANTS THEM TO LEAVE INDIA AND GO TO THEIR OWN COUNTRY.

VIDYAVATI TOLD HER SON HOW THE PEOPLE WERE STRUGGLING FOR THEIR FREEDOM.

LITTLE BHAGAT SINGH RAN TO HIS AUNT.

AUNTIE, DON'T WEEP.

WHEN I GROW UP, I'LL DRIVE THE BRITISH OUT AND BRING UNCLE HOME.

BUT THE BRITISH ARE VERY STRONG. THEY HAVE GUNS AND CANNONS.

DON'T WORRY. I TOO WILL GET GUNS.

MY BRAVE CHILD!

LATER THAT EVENING, AS KISHAN SINGH WAS STROLLING THROUGH HIS ESTATE WITH A FRIEND —

WHAT ARE YOU PLANTING, BHAGAT SINGH?

RIFLES.

RIFLES?

WHY RIFLES?

TO FREE MY COUNTRY.

YES, BHAGAT SINGH. WE NEED RIFLES TO LIBERATE OUR LAND. AND WE NEED BRAVE BOYS LIKE YOU!

BHAGAT SINGH WAS FIRST SENT TO THE VILLAGE SCHOOL. LATER, IN 1916, HE JOINED THE D.A.V. SCHOOL AT LAHORE. HE WAS LOOKED UPON BY HIS FRIENDS AS A LEADER.

EASY ARE UTTERANCES BUT DIFFICULT IS THE SERVICE OF THE NATION. FOR THE PATH OF PATRIOTISM HAS COUNTLESS TORMENTS.

BHAGAT, WHY DO YOU ALWAYS SING THIS SONG?

BECAUSE IT USED TO BE SHAHEED KARTAR SINGH SARABHA'S FAVOURITE SONG!

BHAGAT SINGH WORSHIPPED KARTAR SINGH SARABHA WHO HAD DIED A MARTYR AT TWENTY.

HE IS MY HERO.

IN 1919, WHEN BHAGAT SINGH WAS TWELVE YEARS OLD, THE GOVERNMENT PASSED THE INFAMOUS ROWLATT ACT.

BHAGAT SINGH, WHAT IS THIS ROWLATT ACT? DO YOU KNOW?

I AM TOLD IT EMPOWERS THE GOVERNMENT TO SEND A MAN TO JAIL...

...WITHOUT A TRIAL. NO COURT, NO JUDGE. JUST PICK THE MAN UP AND LOCK HIM IN.

BHAGAT SINGH, YOU KNOW SO MUCH ABOUT THE POLICE AND JAILS!

THAT'S NOT SURPRISING. MY FATHER AND UNCLES WERE IN JAIL. THEIR CRIME? THEY LOVED OUR MOTHERLAND AS SHAHEED KARTAR SINGH DID.

UNDER THE LEADERSHIP OF GANDHIJI, PEOPLE THROUGH-OUT THE COUNTRY PROTESTED AGAINST THE ROWLATT ACT WITH DEMONSTRATIONS AND MEETINGS.

VANDE MATARAM!

AT ONE SUCH MEETING HELD AT JALLIANWALLA BAGH, IN AMRITSAR —

IT WAS A MASSACRE THAT SHOCKED THE COUNTRY.

HUNDREDS OF PEOPLE HAVE BEEN KILLED AND MANY MORE INJURED.

HOW...HOW COULD GENERAL DYER FIRE AT UNARMED PEOPLE?

JALLIANWALLA BAGH! THE HOLY PLACE ANOINTED WITH THE BLOOD OF PATRIOTS! I MUST GO THERE ON A PILGRIMAGE.

BHAGAT SINGH VISITED JALLIANWALLA BAGH.

GOD! THIS WAS A DEATH-TRAP!

THE BULLETS EMBEDDED IN THESE WALLS WILL REMAIN HERE FOREVER — A MEMORIAL TO THE MARTYRS.

BHAGAT SINGH COLLECTED SOME OF THE RED EARTH.

THIS EARTH SHALL INSPIRE ME TO SACRIFICE EVERY-THING FOR THE CAUSE.

THE MASSACRE AT JALLIANWALLA BAGH STIRRED THE CONSCIENCE OF THE NATION. GANDHIJI LAUNCHED THE NON-COOPERATION MOVEMENT.

GANDHIJI HAS GIVEN A CALL TO STOP PAYING TAXES AND TO BOYCOTT SCHOOLS AND COLLEGES AIDED BY THE GOVERNMENT.

HE'S RIGHT. WE SHOULD HAVE NO TRUCK WITH THIS ALIEN GOVERNMENT.

BHAGAT SINGH JOINED THE NATIONAL COLLEGE FOUNDED BY PATRIOTIC CITIZENS. IT WAS HERE THAT HE CAME INTO CONTACT WITH SUKHDEV.

WHAT ARE YOU READING?

A BOOK ON THE HISTORY OF REVOLUTION.

DO YOU THINK WE WILL HAVE A REVOLUTION HERE IN INDIA?

YES. WHEN WE SUCCEED IN AROUSING THE PEOPLE.

7

HOW WILL YOU DO THAT? OUR PEOPLE ARE ILLITERATE. AND THEY FIND LONG SPEECHES TIRESOME.

I KNOW WHAT THEY LIKE MOST—PLAYS AND MUSIC.

BHAGAT SINGH BEGAN TO ACT IN PLAYS LIKE 'RANA PRATAP' STAGED BY THE NATIONAL DRAMATIC CLUB.

DEFENDING ONE'S MOTHERLAND IS A SACRED TASK. WE'LL DO IT TO THE LAST DROP OF OUR BLOOD. NO SACRIFICE IS TOO BIG FOR FREEDOM.

THEN ONE DAY—

WHAT'S THE MATTER, BHAGAT?

MY FATHER WANTS ME TO GET MARRIED TO PLEASE MY GRANDMOTHER. THIS IS THE SECOND LETTER FROM HIM ON THE SUBJECT.

WHAT WILL BE YOUR ANSWER?

THAT AS LONG AS MY COUNTRY IS HELD IN SLAVERY, THE ONLY BRIDE I WILL EMBRACE IS DEATH.

BUT BHAGAT, YOUR GRAND-MOTHER WILL NOT...

I KNOW. THAT'S WHY I HAVE DECIDED TO RUN AWAY.

BHAGAT SINGH WENT TO KANPUR AND MET GANESH SHANKAR VIDYARTHI, A GREAT PATRIOT.

SIR, I HAVE COME TO KANPUR TO ESCAPE GETTING MARRIED. I HAVE BUT ONE PASSION—TO SEE MY COUNTRY FREE!

YOUR PASSION IS LIKE THAT OF THE MOTH FOR THE FLAME. IT COULD PROVE FATAL.

I AM NOT UNAWARE OF THAT, SIR.

AND BHAGAT SINGH BEGAN TO WORK FOR VIDYARTHI'S PRATAP PRESS WHICH SPECIALISED IN NATIONALIST LITERATURE.

HE JOINED THE HINDUSTAN REPUBLIC ASSOCIATION.

WE MUST EDUCATE OUR PEOPLE ON THE NEED FOR FREEDOM.

LEAVE THAT TO US, SIR.

BHAGAT SINGH DID NOT WASTE ANY TIME. ONE DUSSERA DAY, HE AND HIS FIVE COMPANIONS ATTENDED A LOCAL FAIR AND BEGAN TO DISTRIBUTE LEAFLETS.

WAKE UP MY BROTHERS... WAKE UP... READ THIS...

SOON THEY COLLECTED A HUGE CROWD. UNFORTUNATELY, THIS ATTRACTED THE ATTENTION OF A FEW POLICEMEN IN PLAIN CLOTHES.

YOU WANT TO WAKE UP YOUR FELLOW COUNTRYMEN, DO YOU?

THEY HAVE CAUGHT TWO OF OUR FRIENDS.

DON'T WORRY.

BHAGAT SINGH FLUNG THE BUNCH OF LEAFLETS IN THE OPPOSITE DIRECTION.

WHEN THE CROWD MADE A BEE-LINE FOR THEM, HE WENT TO THE POLICEMEN.

LOOK! THOSE MISCHIEF-MONGERS ARE STILL DISTRIBUTING THE LEAFLETS.

ALMOST ALL THE POLICEMEN RUSHED TO THE OTHER SIDE TO ARREST THE 'CULPRITS'!

ONLY TWO OF THEM ARE LEFT TO GUARD OUR FRIENDS.

THE NEXT MOMENT —

WHY DON'T YOU GO AND HELP YOUR FRIENDS TO ARREST THE MISCREANTS?

AS BHAGAT SINGH AND HIS FRIENDS SPED AWAY —

WE HAVE BEEN DUPED! CHASE THEM!

WE ARE BEING CHASED.

THIS SHOULD STOP THEM.

AS ANTICIPATED, THE FRIGHTENED POLICEMEN GAVE UP THE CHASE.

BHAGAT SINGH'S STAY IN KANPUR CAME TO AN ABRUPT END. HE HAD TO LEAVE FOR LAHORE. HIS GRANDMOTHER WAS SERIOUSLY ILL.

YOU CAN GO HOME WITHOUT HESITATION. YOUR FATHER HAS SENT WORD THAT YOU WILL NOT BE ASKED TO GET MARRIED.

BHAGAT SINGH RETURNED TO LAHORE AND NURSED HIS GRANDMOTHER WITH GREAT CARE AND LOVE...

...AND SHE SOON RECOVERED.

THOSE WERE THE DAYS WHEN THE SIKHS HAD LAUNCHED A PROTEST MOVEMENT AGAINST THE BRITISH FOR DEPOSING RIPUDAMAN SINGH, THE MAHARAJA OF NABHA.

BHAGAT, SOME SIKH JATHAS ON THEIR MARCH TO JAITO WILL BE STOPPING AT OUR VILLAGE. I WANT YOU TO LOOK AFTER THEIR COMFORTS.

I WILL LEAVE FOR BANGA IMMEDIATELY.

AT THE VILLAGE, HOWEVER —

IF WE HONOUR THE SIKH JATHAS, WE WILL BE INVITING THE WRATH OF THE GOVERNMENT.

THAT SHOULD NOT DETER US FROM OFFERING OUR HOSPITALITY TO THE GUESTS, UNCLE.

BHAGAT SINGH HAD HIS WAY. LATER —

GOD BLESS YOU, SON. YOU HAVE TAKEN GREAT PAINS TO MAKE OUR STAY COMFORTABLE.

BUT THE GOVERNMENT, AS EXPECTED, WAS ANNOYED.

YOU'D BETTER RUN, BROTHER. WARRANTS HAVE BEEN ISSUED FOR YOUR ARREST.

THANK YOU FOR THE TIP.

BHAGAT SINGH FLED TO LAHORE.

AT LAHORE, BHAGAT SINGH AND HIS FRIENDS FORMED AN ASSOCIATION CALLED "NAV JAWAN BHARAT SABHA".

I PROMISE TO PLACE THE INTERESTS OF MY COUNTRY ABOVE THOSE OF MY COMMUNITY...

NAV JAWAN BHARAT SABHA

THE SABHA WORKED FOR PATRIOTIC CAUSES LIKE THE SWADESHI MOVEMENT.

THE SABHA OBSERVED MARTYRS' DAY IN MEMORY OF RAMPRASAD BISMIL, ASHFAQULLAH KHAN AND OTHER REVOLUTIONARIES WHO HAD BEEN HANGED BY THE GOVERNMENT.

BISMILJI AND ASHFAQULLAH DIED AT THE GALLOWS, SMILING. OUR HOMAGE TO THEM CAN ONLY BE IN CARRYING ON THEIR FIGHT FOR FREEDOM.

IN SEPTEMBER 1928, REVOLUTIONARIES FROM DIFFERENT PARTS OF INDIA MET IN DELHI. CHANDRA SHEKHAR AZAD, THE HEAD OF THE HINDUSTAN REPUBLICAN ASSOCIATION, INITIATED THE DISCUSSION.

THE COUNTRY IS RESTLESS. FREEDOM IS TO BE WON, NOT TO BE BEGGED FOR. WE MUST ORGANISE OURSELVES ON A WAR FOOTING.

I AGREE WITH YOU, AZAD.

AT THE CONCLUSION OF THE MEETING—

NOW LET'S DISPERSE. WE MUST BE CAREFUL. THE POLICE KNOW THAT WE ARE MEETING IN DELHI ALTHOUGH THEY DON'T KNOW EXACTLY WHERE.

THEN, DRESSED AS A POLICE CONSTABLE, BHAGAT SINGH LEFT FOR LAHORE. AT THE DELHI RAILWAY STATION A POLICE OFFICIAL ENTERED HIS COMPARTMENT.

WHAT IS YOUR NAME? WHICH POLICE STATION ARE YOU ATTACHED TO AND WHY ARE YOU HERE?

SIR, I AM KARTAR SINGH FROM NIHAL SINGH WALA POLICE STATION. I ESCORTED SOME PRISONERS TO DELHI.

SHOW ME YOUR RAILWAY PASS.

MY COLLEAGUE HAS GONE TO GET IT ENDORSED.

I SEE.

I DON'T THINK HE BELIEVES ME.

THE POLICE OFFICIAL LEFT THE COMPARTMENT.

HE'S SURE TO CHECK WITH THE BOOKING OFFICE.

BHAGAT SINGH ENTERED ANOTHER COMPARTMENT AND LOCKED HIMSELF UP IN THE LAVATORY. AS THE TRAIN BEGAN TO LEAVE THE STATION, THE POLICE OFFICIAL RETURNED WITH A FEW CONSTABLES...

...AND BOARDED IT.

THE ROGUE MUST BE SOMEWHERE HERE. MAKE A THOROUGH SEARCH.

WHEN THE TRAIN REACHED THE NEXT STATION—

WE HAVE LOOKED EVERYWHERE, SIR. WE CAN'T FIND HIM.

LITTLE DID THEY REALISE THAT THE MAN THEY WERE LOOKING FOR WAS SEATED RIGHT THERE WITH A COPY OF THE GITA IN HIS HAND.

ON HIS RETURN TO LAHORE, BHAGAT SINGH CALLED A MEETING OF THE NAV JAWAN BHARAT SABHA.

WHAT SHOULD BE OUR STAND ON THE SIMON COMMISSION?

IT DOES NOT HAVE A SINGLE INDIAN MEMBER ON IT!

THE SIMON COMMISSION WAS APPOINTED BY THE BRITISH TO STUDY THE POLITICAL SITUATION IN THE COUNTRY.

WE MUST JOIN THE ALL-PARTIES PROCESSION AGAINST THE VISIT OF THE SIMON COMMISSION.

ON OCTOBER 30, 1928, A HUGE PROCESSION WAS TAKEN OUT BY LALA LAJPAT RAI, THE GREAT LEADER FROM THE PUNJAB.

GO BACK! SIMON COMMISSION GO BACK!

SIMON GO BACK

INDIA FOR INDIANS.

A POLICE PARTY STOPPED THE PROCESSION NEAR THE RAILWAY STATION.

TURN BACK AND DISPERSE.

BUT LALAJI MARCHED AHEAD. THEN THE POLICE RESORTED TO A LATHI CHARGE.

IT IS BARBAROUS TO ATTACK UNARMED, AND NON-VIOLENT PEOPLE.

ONE LATHI CAME DOWN ON THE UMBRELLA WHICH LALAJI WAS HOLDING.

NO!

BHAGAT SINGH AND HIS COMRADES THREW A CORDON ROUND LALAJI. YET HE WAS HIT ON HIS SHOULDER AND CHEST.

LATER IN THE EVENING —

DO YOU KNOW WHAT LALAJI SAID?

YES, I DO. THE LION OF THE PUNJAB ROARED: I DECLARE THAT EVERY BLOW THEY HURLED AT US DROVE ONE MORE NAIL INTO THE COFFIN OF THE EMPIRE.

LALAJI NEVER RECOVERED FROM THE BLOWS HE RECEIVED. HE DIED TWO WEEKS LATER.

LALAJI'S NON-VIOLENCE WAS REWARDED WITH FATAL BLOWS.

THIS GOVERNMENT UNDERSTANDS ONLY ONE LANGUAGE — BLOOD FOR BLOOD.

CHANDRA SHEKHAR AZAD NOW ARRIVED IN LAHORE TO DISCUSS PLANS FOR REVENGE.

FRIENDS, WE ARE FIGHTING A WAR OF INDEPENDENCE. THE BRITISH HAVE SOLDIERS, WEAPONS AND UNLIMITED RESOURCES. WE HAVE ONLY THE SPIRIT OF SACRIFICE.

TO AVENGE THE DEATH OF ONE INDIAN, TEN ENGLISHMEN MUST DIE. AND SINCE SCOTT, THE SUPERINTENDENT OF POLICE RAISED HIS LATHI AGAINST LALAJI, HE SHALL DIE FIRST.

ON DECEMBER 17, 1928, BHAGAT SINGH AND HIS COMRADE, RAJGURU TOOK THEIR POSITIONS NEAR THE POLICE STATION.

JAIGOPAL WILL SIGNAL TO US AS SOON AS SCOTT COMES OUT.

POLICE STATION

D.A.V. COL

JAIGOPAL WHO HAD STATIONED HIMSELF JUST OPPOSITE THE POLICE STATION WAS PRETENDING TO REPAIR HIS BICYCLE.

LOOK! THAT OFFICER IS WALKING TOWARDS THE MOTOR-CYCLE. IS HE SCOTT?

17

YES, HE IS OUR MAN. JAI GOPAL HAS SIGNALLED.

TAKE AIM, THEN.

EVEN AS THE WHITE MAN WAS STARTING THE MOTOR-CYCLE, HE WAS HIT BY A VOLLEY OF BULLETS.

AS BHAGAT SINGH AND RAJGURU RAN TOWARDS THE D.A.V. COLLEGE JUST OPPOSITE THE POLICE STATION, THEY WERE CHASED BY A POLICE CONSTABLE.

KEEP RUNNING. AZAD AND SUKHDEV WILL TAKE CARE OF HIM.

AZAD DID NOT FAIL THEM. HE WAS READY.

ONE STEP FORWARD AND I'LL SHOOT. GO BACK!

THE CONSTABLE IGNORED THE WARNING AND PAID FOR IT WITH HIS LIFE.

MEANWHILE, BHAGAT SINGH AND RAJGURU HAD REACHED THE QUADRANGLE OF THE COLLEGE.

THEY WENT UP TO THE FIRST FLOOR...

...ENTERED A ROOM...

...SCRAMBLED OUT OF THE WINDOW...

...SLITHERED DOWN A WATER-PIPE AND...

...MOUNTING THE BICYCLE LEFT THERE FOR THEM...

... GOT AWAY.

LATER, THEY REALISED THAT THE MAN THEY HAD KILLED WAS SAUNDERS, THE ASSISTANT SUPERINTENDENT OF POLICE AND NOT SCOTT.

NEVER MIND. HE IS ALSO A WHITE POLICE OFFICIAL, A BRITISH IMPERIALIST.

WE MUST MAKE THAT CLEAR TO THE PEOPLE.

ON THE FOLLOWING DAY, NOTICES APPEARED ALL OVER THE CITY.

HINDUSTAN SOCIALIST REPUBLICAN ASSOCIATION

WE REGRET THAT A WHITE MAN HAD TO BE KILLED, BUT HE WAS PART AND PARCEL OF THE INHUMAN, UNJUST BRITISH RULE WHICH HAS TO BE DESTROY-ED...

THE WHOLE OF THE PUNJAB RESOUNDED WITH THE NEWS.

LALAJI'S MURDER HAS BEEN AVENGED!

WHOEVER IS RESPONSIBLE FOR IT, HAS ERASED THE STIGMA OF NATIONAL INSULT.

MEANWHILE, POLICE GUARDS KEPT WATCH OVER ALL ROADS LEADING OUT OF LAHORE...

...AS WELL AS AT THE RAILWAY STATION.

WATCH OUT FOR THE CRIMINALS! ONE OF THEM IS A YOUNG SIKH.

YES, SIR.

AS THE ATTENTION OF THE POLICE WAS FOCUSSED ON THOSE WHO WERE TRAVELLING ALONE, THEY HARDLY NOTICED THE TONGA WHICH BROUGHT A PROSPEROUS LOOKING FAMILY TO THE STATION.

THE ELEGANTLY DRESSED SAHIB WALKED UP TO THE BOOKING OFFICE WINDOW. HIS WIFE AND CHILD AND A SERVANT FOLLOWED.

THE SAHIB BOUGHT THE TICKETS AND THE POLICE LET THE PARTY ENTER THE PLATFORM.

THE SAHIB AND HIS WIFE BOARDED A FIRST CLASS COMPARTMENT, AND THE SERVANT, A THIRD CLASS COMPARTMENT.

THE BIRDS HAD FLOWN! THE SAHIB WAS NONE OTHER THAN BHAGAT SINGH WHO HAD SHAVED OFF HIS BEARD TO AVOID DETECTION; THE WOMAN WHO POSED AS HIS WIFE WAS DURGA BHABHI, THE WIFE OF A REVOLUTIONARY, BHAGWATI CHARAN; AND THE MAN WHO ACCOMPANIED THEM AS THEIR SERVANT WAS RAJGURU!

CHANDRASHEKHAR AZAD GOT AWAY TO MATHURA, POSING AS A SADHU.

BHAGAT SINGH MEANWHILE HAD TRAVELLED EASTWARDS TO CALCUTTA. THERE HE MET JATIN DAS, A REVOLUTIONARY.

JATIN, TEACH ME HOW TO MAKE BOMBS. WE NEED THEM.

I WILL GLADLY HELP YOU.

LATER, A BOMB MANUFACTURING CENTRE WAS OPENED IN AGRA. AT A MEETING HELD THERE, THE REVOLUTIONARIES DISCUSSED THEIR FUTURE COURSE OF ACTION.

THE GOVERNMENT IS BENT ON GETTING THE TRADE DISPUTE BILL AND THE PUBLIC SAFETY BILL PASSED.

THESE BILLS WERE MEANT TO SUPPRESS THE LABOUR CLASS AND EMPOWERED THE GOVERN-MENT TO JAIL ANYONE WITHOUT GIVING A REASON.

THE BRITISH WANT TO CRUSH US...THE EYES OF BRITISH AND INDIAN MEMBERS OF THE ASSEMBLY WILL HAVE TO BE OPENED.

BUT HOW?

THE DAY THE BILL IS INTRODUCED, BOMBS SHOULD BE THROWN. WE WILL MAKE A NOISE LOUD ENOUGH TO BE HEARD BY THE DEAF.

A GOOD IDEA! BUT MAKE SURE THAT THE BOMB HURTS NOBODY. WE MUST MAKE PLANS TO ENTER THE ASSEMBLY, THROW THE BOMB AND ESCAPE...

NO!

THE ONE WHO THROWS THE BOMB SHOULD COURT ARREST. LATER HE SHOULD USE THE COURT AS A PLATFORM TO EXPRESS OUR IDEOLOGY... TO ROUSE PUBLIC OPINION. OUR ARREST AND SUBSEQUENT TRIAL WILL ACT AS A DAILY REMINDER TO THE PEOPLE OF THE OBJECTIVES THEY HAVE BEFORE THEM.

SO ON APRIL 8, 1929 WHEN THE CENTRAL ASSEMBLY MET TO DISCUSS THE BILLS, BHAGAT SINGH AND HIS COMPANION, BATUKESHWAR DUTT, STOOD UP IN THE VISITORS' GALLERY.

INQUILAB ZINDABAD!

THE BOMB WAS THROWN. IT HURT NOBODY. SOME LEAFLETS TOO WERE THROWN.

THE TWO REVOLUTIONARIES CONTINUED TO SHOUT SLOGANS TILL THE POLICE CAME FOR THEM. THEY DID NOT RESIST ARREST.

YOU ARE UNDER ARREST.

DON'T WORRY. WE SHALL TELL THE WHOLE WORLD WE DID IT.

BHAGAT SINGH AND DUTT WERE TAKEN TO THE POLICE STATION. ON THE WAY THEY PASSED THE TONGA CARRYING DURGA BHABHI, HER HUSBAND AND THEIR LITTLE SON.

LAMME CHACHA!*

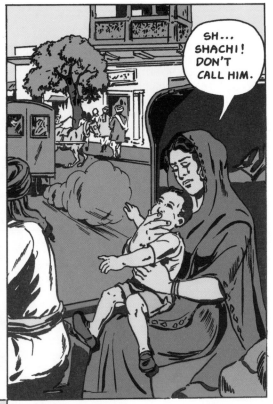

SH... SHACHI! DON'T CALL HIM.

LATER IN THE MAGISTRATE'S COURT, ASAF ALI, THE LAWYER, READ OUT THE STATEMENT PREPARED BY BHAGAT SINGH.

WE DROPPED THE BOMB ...TO REGISTER OUR PROTEST ON BEHALF OF THOSE WHO HAD NO OTHER MEANS LEFT TO GIVE EXPRESSION TO THEIR HEART-RENDING AGONY...

...OUR SOLE PURPOSE WAS TO MAKE THE DEAF HEAR AND GIVE THE HEEDLESS A TIMELY WARNING.

THE TWO REVOLUTIONARIES WERE SENTENCED TO TRANSPORTATION FOR LIFE. THEY FILED AN APPEAL IN THE HIGH COURT.

GENERAL DYER KILLED HUNDREDS OF PERSONS IN JALLIANWALLA BAGH. HE WAS GIVEN LAKHS OF RUPEES AS A REWARD BY HIS COUNTRYMEN.

IN CONTRAST, WE THROW A WEAK BOMB ENSURING THAT NO ONE IS HURT. WE ARE TRIED AND GIVEN A LIFE SENTENCE.

OUR MOTIVE WAS NOT TO KILL, BUT TO MAKE OUR IDEALS HEARD AND ACCEPTED.

AS EXPECTED, THE HIGH COURT UPHELD THE JUDGEMENT OF THE SESSIONS COURT.

LATER BHAGAT SINGH WAS SHIFTED TO THE LAHORE CENTRAL JAIL.

I WOULD LIKE TO HAVE SOME BOOKS...

BOOKS? DO YOU THINK THIS IS A LIBRARY?

THAT NIGHT —

WHAT IS THIS? THIS FOOD IS UNFIT FOR HUMAN CONSUMPTION.

YOU ARE A CRIMINAL. BE GRATEFUL FOR WHAT YOU ARE GIVEN.

BHAGAT SINGH WAS SHOCKED AT THE TREATMENT METED OUT TO POLITICAL PRISONERS.

FRIENDS, OUTSIDE THE JAIL WE FIGHT FOR FREEDOM. INSIDE THE JAIL WE MUST FIGHT FOR OUR HONOUR.

WE ARE PRISONERS BUT OUR HUMAN DIGNITY MUST BE RESPECTED. LET US GO ON A HUNGER STRIKE IN PROTEST.

WE ARE WITH YOU.

THE GOVERNMENT DID RESPOND BUT NOT BEFORE JATIN DAS, ONE OF THOSE ON A HUNGER STRIKE, DIED A MARTYR.

MEANWHILE THE GOVERNMENT HAD CAST ITS NET FAR AND WIDE. SEVERAL REVOLUTIONARIES HAD BEEN ARRESTED. BHAGAT SINGH AND HIS COMRADES, RAJGURU AND SUKHDEV WERE TRIED FOR SAUNDERS' MURDER. KISHAN SINGH CAME RUSHING TO THE JAIL.

MY SON, I WILL GET THE BEST LAWYER AVAILABLE TO DEFEND YOU AND SECURE YOUR RELEASE.

NO, FATHER. THE GOVERNMENT, ITS LAW COURTS AND VERDICTS MEAN NOTHING TO ME

KISHAN SINGH LEFT THE JAIL WITH A HEAVY HEART.

MY SON DOESN'T KNOW WHAT IS GOOD FOR HIM. I WILL SUBMIT A PETITION TO THE GOVERNMENT...

IN HIS PETITION KISHAN SINGH PLEADED THAT HIS SON WAS NOT IN LAHORE AT THE TIME OF SAUNDERS' MURDER. BHAGAT SINGH REACTED SHARPLY TO HIS FATHER'S MOVE.

MY LIFE IS NOT SO PRECIOUS... AS YOU MAY THINK IT TO BE...

...YOU'VE ALWAYS BEEN A DAUNTLESS FREEDOM-FIGHTER. WHAT MAKES YOU WEAK NOW?

MY SON, FORGIVE ME!

ON OCTOBER 7, 1930, THE STATE ADVOCATE CALLED ON BHAGAT SINGH.

SARDAR, I'M SORRY. THE COURT HAS AWARDED YOU THE DEATH SENTENCE.

YES. SO I'VE HEARD. BUT NO ONE NEED FEEL SORRY FOR ME.

YOU ARE BRAVE. BUT TO DIE AT THIS YOUNG AGE...! I ADVISE YOU TO SUBMIT A MERCY PETITION.

THERE IS NO NEED.

WHY NOT?

IT IS BETTER TO DIE BRAVELY THAN TO CRINGE BEFORE THE ENEMY.

I AM THE MOTH OF THE FLAME OF LIBERTY.

BHAGAT SINGH'S MOTHER, VIDYAVATI, WAS EQUALLY BRAVE. WHEN SHE MET HER SON IN JAIL —

SON, DEATH CLAIMS EVERYONE. YET DYING FOR A NOBLE CAUSE IS THE PRIVILEGE GIVEN TO A CHOSEN FEW. I AM PROUD OF YOU.

BUT HIS YOUNGEST BROTHER, KULTAR SINGH, COULD NOT WITHHOLD HIS TEARS. LATER, BHAGAT SINGH WROTE HIM A LETTER.

IT PAINED ME TO SEE TEARS IN YOUR EYES TODAY...DON'T LOSE HEART...WHAT MORE CAN I WRITE?

BHAGAT SINGH WAS TO BE HANGED ON MARCH 23, 1931. WHEN THE JAILOR WENT TO HIS CELL, BHAGAT SINGH WAS READING A BOOK ON THE LIFE OF LENIN, THE GREAT RUSSIAN REVOLUTIONARY.

SARDAR, WE HAVE COME TO LEAD YOU TO THE GALLOWS.

JUST A MOMENT PLEASE. LET ONE REVOLUTIONARY MEET ANOTHER.

A FEW SECONDS LATER, HE CLOSED THE BOOK AND GOT UP.

SUKHDEV AND RAJGURU WERE BROUGHT FROM THEIR CELLS. AT 7.00 P.M. THE LAST JOURNEY BEGAN. BHAGAT SINGH BURST INTO SONG.

YOU WILL KILL US BUT NOT THE PATRIOTISM IN US. THE FRAGRANCE OF FREEDOM SHALL RISE FROM OUR PYRES.

HEARING THE SONG, OTHER PRISONERS IN THE JAIL RAISED PATRIOTIC CRIES.

INQUILAB ZINDABAD!

UP WITH THE NATIONAL FLAG.

THE THREE REVOLUTIONARIES MARCHED UP TO THE GALLOWS, WATCHED BY THE OFFICIALS. THEN BHAGAT SINGH TURNED TO THE BRITISH DEPUTY COMMISSIONER.

WELL, MR. MAGISTRATE, YOU ARE LUCKY. TODAY YOU SHALL SEE HOW INDIANS EMBRACE DEATH WITH PLEASURE FOR THE SAKE OF THEIR SUPREME IDEAL.

THEN THE LAHORE JAIL RESOUNDED WITH A POWERFUL CRY—

INQUILAB ZINDABAD!

THE VOICE WAS STILLED FOR A MOMENT WHEN THE HANGMAN PULLED THE ROPE. BUT THE CRY WAS TAKEN UP BY MILLIONS OF INDIANS.

INQUILAB ZINDABAD!

INQUILAB ZINDABAD

"THE LESSON WHICH WE SHOULD LEARN FROM BHAGAT SINGH IS TO DIE IN A MANLY AND BOLD MANNER SO THAT INDIA MIGHT LIVE," WROTE JAWAHARLAL NEHRU OF THIS VALIANT YOUNG MARTYR.

21 Inspiring Stories of Courage

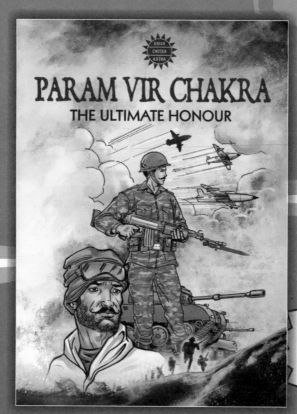

To buy this product, visit your nearest bookstore
or buy online at **www.amarchitrakatha.com** or call: **022-49188881/2/3/4**